Catching Meara

McKenna Clan Series Book One

Christine Young

Chapter One

Meara had been seconds from revelation, mere seconds. Now quivering with terror, she huddled in the corner of her electrified office while lights flashed and popped all around her, knowing there was no where to run. Monitors flashed and burst, exploding and sending shards of liquid fire into the air. A cop entered the small room, his arms stretched forward, gun in both hands and a flashlight on top of his gun.

Three more cops followed behind. No, they were government agents. The logo printed in white across their chest announced their profession.

Bright lights swept the room in a slow steady arc, searching for her. Finally resting on her face, she shielded her eyes. Smoke from the crucified computers filled the cubicle, making the agents choke. Sweat from fear beaded on her forehead, and her heart lurched to her throat. She closed her hands over her heart as if she could slow the furious beating.

"Hewitt, check this out. There might be more than this one. Barrister go search through the other rooms."

"Right, McKenna."

"My name is Jace McKenna," the man said as he approached cautiously, kicking debris from under foot until he stood above her. "Put your hands in the air."

His voice held so much authority and sounded so calm. For a moment she thought he meant to reassure then she remembered she was his prisoner. Well, she would be as soon as she complied with his demands.

Jace, appeared dark, dangerous, handsome and tall, she noted at first. Very tall, which was hard to miss, since she was skinny and short. His eyes were an amber color with a hint of green. He towered over her. Beneath the deceiving bulkiness of his bulletproof vest, she observed next, his shoulders were very broad, and though his hips were lean, his thighs, tightly hugged by his jeans, were muscled and powerful.

His hair was blacker than the midnight sky, nearly indigo with its sheen, his amber eyes were cast into a rugged face that appeared naturally tanned. He was probably somewhere in his late twenties or early thirties. He seemed fierce, alive with a striking tension and a volatile energy that seemed to exude from him.

Shaking, sweat dripping down her face, Meara slowly raised her trembling arms. "D-don't shoot--me, please" She heard the pathetic whimper in her voice as she blinked the stinging sweat from her eyes where it melded with her mascara. Her heart pounded so hard against her chest she was sure it would burst through her ribs.

"Stand up, slowly." He swept the flashlight as well as the gun up and down the length of her body, which had been curled into a tight fetal position.

Rising to her feet, she leaned against the wall behind her, trying to keep her hands up and not fall flat on her face. She wiggled her butt against the wall and inched her way to a standing position. Her life flashed in front of her in a series of leaps and bounds until she saw the faces of her parents.

"Do as he says," they whispered. *"Everything will turn out fine. You'll see. We love you."* Then, just as they appeared, they vanished.

Their faces faded into the smoke and flashing lights. Her eyes open wide, she gazed at her enemy--her jailor. The man who was here to arrest her. Mind games, or was it mind think that her parents used to play with her, teaching her to communicate through thoughts instead of words. She focused on his brain, sending out feelers, trying to read his thoughts and trying to tell him she was no threat.

The next moment he was beside her, grasping one of her arms, and in one swift move he had turned her, both hands were behind her back and handcuffed. Her breath stopped for a moment. The movement had been so sudden she was thrown against the wall. Her face flattened on the smooth surface. Yet she was glad for that because the impact brought her back to the reality of this moment. Her mind cleared for a brief second. For courage she inhaled a swift deep breath.

"You have the right to remain silent..."

She focused on her thoughts, turning inward to a peaceful scene in her mind as he read her rights to her. She liked to imagine a huge meadow filled with colorful wildflowers that would stretch as far as the eye could see. She imagined heat from the sun beating down on her face. Birds chirped in the distance. Swallows soared effortlessly on the wind currents.

"...Anything you say can and will be used against you in a court of law."

He gave her a gentle nudge to send her walking through the still flashing lights and spits of fire. At the touch of his hand on the small of her back, Meara felt a rush of sensations. Nerve endings hit synapse after synapse until her head swam with the swift input of visions. So bright and strange they terrified.

3

She inhaled a sharp gasp of air, wavering unsteadily, and leaned into the man who held her life in his hands. "You, you...you can't touch me." She tried to push away from the feel of his powerful body against hers. Her whisper echoed in the room as a plea for her life, for her very soul. She felt as if possessed but not by the devil, by something intangible, a being she had never encountered before. In the back of her mind she envisioned a large black jaguar.

Incredible and so beautiful.

He seemed to ignore her request and continued walking towards the door, hand still touching her back.

Hewitt and Barrister then a third agent joined them, falling in behind.

"There's no one else here," Barrister said.

Her head pounded and her hair hung in her eyes. She gave her head a little shake in a failed attempt to dislodge her hair from her face and scrambling her vision. The weight and the sensation of his hand seemed to lighten a bit. It seemed as if this being knew she had reached her limit and he wanted to comfort her.

"Don't be afraid," his voice sounded deep dark and dangerous but strangely reassuring. "Everything will be fine."

Slowly she inhaled a long and very deep breath to calm her frazzled nerves. Then she inhaled again.

Falling off the grid had been paramount in her existence since she lost her parents. They had disappeared almost exactly two years ago, and she had plunged into a deep depression. All that kept her sanity in check was her workstation and the soft cathartic hum and buzz that accompanied her in the computer lab. She had taught herself code, and she had become the best of the best. She was an incredible hacker.

"That's why you're here." The whispered words startled her. "I discovered something I wasn't supposed to know." But she didn't

4

identify the code, and she didn't reach the end of her search. She had perhaps been seconds from revelation when her monitor exploded in front of her, and she found refuge in the corner of the tiny room she called home. At the moment of the blast, she knew her work as a hacker was finished. Emptiness engulfed her, filling her mind with pain and sorrow.

The man nodded, his expression grim determination. Yet she sensed a protected vulnerability. His muscles bulged and his rosette tattoo was identical to hers...

What the...

She didn't believe in coincidence. Everything happens for a reason.

His tattoo decorated his bicep just below the line of his t-shirt. When she searched closer, he had more than one rosette. His pants stretched tautly around his legs, hiding nothing, absolutely nothing...

Heat rushed to her cheeks even while they walked through the long corridor to the outside of the building. She needed to get her libido under control or she was going to blurt out her sexual fantasy to this unknown man who seemed to cause the most unusual sensations to clog her brain and her body.

They stepped through the large wooden door, now broken and wobbling on one hinge, to walk outside. Blinding bright sunlight made her squint and groan at the pain. She'd been underground for way too long. If she closed her eyes, the brightness would ease but her problems would not go away.

"Over here," he said, still guiding her, his touch upon her so very light, gentle and comforting.

"She confess?" one of the agents laughed.

Confess what? Declare her incompetence? Even though someone had caught on to what she was about to decipher, she didn't understand what had been right in front of her. But with each thought the screen seemed to grow clearer in her head.

"Oh..."

"I think she's figured it out, McKenna," Barrister said.

"Sounds like you're right." McKenna put his hand on top of her head to keep her from bumping it as she entered the SUV.

Jace. She mulled her captor's name over in her mind. In Native American--Moon. Did he worship the moon? He had found her in an ancient city in the mountains, the Sierra Madre Mountains, just at the border between Texas and Mexico. Not many lived here. The food was sparse. Some hunted and fished, but the main population had long ago abandoned the little town. A friend brought her a meal each day. Since she had found her way here and into the underground lab, she had not stepped outside.

"Where are we going?" They had to have flown in from somewhere. Where did this group call their home? She felt no sadness at leaving. Instead she felt a sense of moving on and starting over. If she didn't wind up in jail, this was a new beginning for her, and she would make the most of any opportunity that might come along.

"City of Angels," he told her with a slight smile. "We'll take the jet home. There is an old runway about five miles north."

She'd lived outside Los Angeles in a little borough with her parents. Meara didn't think she would ever go back to the city. Yet they had been happy. That was a lifetime ago.

The car roared to life. Traffic? None to speak of--so she and the government agents sat in silence. She leaned back, closing her eyes and absorbing the thrum of the engine, the wind against the car and the low tenor of the men's voices rumbling around her. It was strange to be talked about and around but not to.

"I'm a computer geek, not a serial killer. Do I really need the cuffs," Meara asked after the muscles in her arm cramped painfully. Writhing where she sat, she could do nothing to ease the agony.

Jace reached for the key to the handcuffs. "Don't see a reason to keep you in the cuffs," he told her his voice a low purr. "But you'd better behave yourself."

Or what, she wanted to say but didn't.

Unlocking the restraints, he touched her again. Once again all her nerves frayed one strand at a time. Her parents had used the handcuffs for...oh my god...they had cuffed each other to the bed and...

She didn't know the--and. All she remembered was walking into their bedroom one Sunday morning and seeing her mother straddled over her father. Both of her father's arms were manacled to the bed.

Her mother wore this flimsy little black negligee. Her father was moaning and whispering something she didn't understand until they saw her.

"F...!" her father had said then her mother turned toward her, a very unusual expression on her flushed face.

"Jonathan! Then Meara!" she cried out, quickly covering her naked father with a comforter. Before her mother jumped from the bed, she pulled on a cover and wrapped her arm around her six-year-old shoulders. Purposely she escorted her daughter from the room. She remembered feeling intensely curious and filled with questions, but her mother had shushed her and there was nothing more said.

Now she knew what they were up to. She watched enough movies, talked to her girlfriends and read the sex-ed books in school to know about sex--good sex. After that episode she had looked at her parent's bedroom in a different way and always with a smile in her heart when the door was closed.

She stared at Jace. The handcuffs were gone and she rubbed her wrists. He seemed to guess the nature of her distress because he massaged her arms with his strong lean fingers. Suddenly her blood seemed to boil and her core softened with need. She cried out suddenly, very afraid of the sensations sweeping through her.

Despite the fear, Meara wanted this man in the most basic and primal way. She wondered what it would be like to handcuff Jace to her bedposts. She shook the crazy thought from her head and wondered where it had come from. She was so far ahead of herself. She didn't even know this man.

"Is that better?" he asked, his voice soft and filled with concern. "I don't want to hurt you."

Meara's imagination went viral. What a laugh. She was scrawny, her hair was striped with pink and blue coloring--all in the name of rebellion. Her eyes were outlined with black eyeliner and her skin was so pale it tended to look transparent. Her blood red lipstick added to the effect of death. At this moment she could have passed for a vampire except the sun didn't seem to affect her.

And he was Adonis. His skin was a soft brown hue. His hair was short. Would it be soft? His eyes were a deep amber, and when he looked at her, she thought he must surely see inside her soul. He would find so much love as well the emptiness she could vanquish. She sensed emotions emanating from him but couldn't quite get a handle on his thoughts.

A short time later they arrived at the airport. Driving on the little used tarmac, they reached the jet and boarded. The transport was luxurious. With thick carpets and plush seats, she thought she was surely in heaven.

Jace pointed for her to sit. He took a seat opposite her. The others settled in and made themselves, she assumed, comfortable. Minutes later the jet took off.

"What's going to happen to me?"

Jace rubbed his jaw, seeming to think, "You are one of the best hackers in the world. I'm talking top two or three. No one is better than you."

All this was true, but she'd never heard those statistics quite like he quoted them. "So..." she shrugged, cocking her head to the side then pushing her hair from her eyes. "I could use a bath. Am I going straight to jail?"

"Depends," he said, staring at her as if he wanted to devour her. His dimple became very apparent as he seemed to fight back a smile.

"You don't understand anything." Lord, but he smelled good-a bit of evergreen and a tangy scent that reminded her of citrus. She felt her cheeks grow hot and her insides boil.

"Enlighten me." He smiled, showing even white teeth and a twinkle in his eyes.

"I would wither and die in jail." She licked her lips then swallowed as everything inside fluttered crazily.

"It's not up to me. It's all up to you."

"I have a choice?" she asked, suddenly eager to find she might have another possibility than a bed behind bars.

"You have two choices."

~ * ~

Inside the twenty story brick and mortar building in Los Angeles, the air was artificially cooled. Jace strode through the hallways with Meara at his side. When he'd first seen her, he'd inhaled her soft scent reveling in her beauty. Her hair shone in various colors of pink, blue and blond in the exploding and flashing lights of the room where he'd found her. Her cheeks flushed a beautiful shade of crimson as if in the throes of passion. It didn't matter she was thin. It suited her. When he saw her, smelled her, he knew. The sight of her made his groin tighten painfully behind his zipper. He needed to see her lips swell and redden after he had expertly and meticulously kissed her.

He hoped she would take the job she was about to be offered. If she chose more rebellion, she'd spend the rest of her life in jail. He couldn't live with himself if she was locked up. She was just too frail for prison life, and he knew she'd wither and die there. Besides, from the moment he scented her, he knew she was his mate. He'd move heaven and earth to make sure she understood she was his forever.

He opened the door for Meara and ushered her into Colton's office. Colton rose and held out his hand to her. She turned and looked at him, eyes wide, but she didn't show any fear. When she turned back to face Colton, she accepted the gesture and with a stiff back, she shook hands.

"Colton, this is Meara, our hacker."

Colton was the team leader. He had dark hair and steel blue eyes. He laughed easily except when they were on a case. When they were working, he never smiled, the seriousness of the situation seeming to pervade all of his thoughts.

Jace relaxed slightly. He knew about Meara, had read her file and he understood she was capable of anything when a computer was involved. Her feisty nature intrigued him, and he felt himself inexorably drawn to her. Cleaned up she would be beautiful. Her eyes were wide blue pools of intelligence, and her pert little nose he guessed would be turned skyward whenever she disagreed with him. A genuineness encompassed her. When he'd touched her, even to handcuff her, blood roared in his ears and his body hardened. His feelings were intense. Inside his jaguar growled low, pacing within his head. His nerves synapses snapped and popped when he touched her. So he shook the cuffs off and concentrated on learning more about her.

"Nice to finely meet you, Meara Thorton. I've been--intrigued by your work." One of Colton's eyebrows rose, a gesture he was well known for.

"How do you know about me?" Meara rested her hands on the chair in front of Colton's desk.

"Oh, my dear girl, we've been watching you for a year now. Ever since you hacked into a top-secret communication between the Russians and us. We need your expertise. And we're hoping..."

"You must have me mixed up with someone else," she interrupted him then blew a piece of pink hair away from her eyes.

"No."

It didn't appear she was going to come over to this side easily. She had so many barriers built up around her a wrecking ball would have difficulty breaking her down. And for almost two years she'd been living in a jail cell of her own making. She should be jumping for joy at this opportunity. His cat wanted to know her better, needed to memorize her scent.

"Trust is so elusive," she pointed out. "I don't like big brother watching over my shoulder." Her arms trembled. She stepped back, rubbing them as if she could make the quivering stop.

"One mistake and any agreement we make here today will be null and void." Colton's fingers drummed the desk. His lips thinned perceptibly. Jace knew that look very well. Colton was a stern taskmaster, but he had a caring side to him also. If Meara agreed to his deal, he would move heaven and earth to make her comfortable.

Sweat beaded on Jace's forehead. He understood the investment he already had in this tiny little lady. *"You understand nothing."* His cat

11

needed to get to know her better, perhaps intimately if she would allow it. His thoughts jolted inside. Too much too soon. Why would he jump to thoughts of intimacy? Because she was his mate and the sooner she knew it, the easier life would be for both of them.

"If I agree, what then? Where will I live? My duties?" For a moment she seemed to consider Colton's offer. "I don't want to be in any danger. And...I hate guns, no, I loathe them. I'm terrified of shadows on the walls. I don't think I would fit in at all."

She was rambling, seeming to try and convince herself. But the alternatives weren't good.

"You will be working for the profilers; Jace, me, and a team of five others. You have already met two of those five. You won't be in the field or in danger." Colton rose from his chair. "Would you like to see your lab?"

"Of course." Her eyes lit up the room, and her smile gave Jace more ideas of kissing her lips until she grinned for him not a room full of computers. Damn it, the last thing he needed was to scare his mate. It took a hell of a lot of self-control to fake his anger at the men she smiled at.

My soul mate, my mate for all eternity.

Jace wanted to reach out and give her a hug of reassurance. She was trying so damn hard and for what? She didn't even know. If she guessed how much his team wanted her, she'd be smiling from ear to ear. No, the team needed her skills, her expertise and her intuitive thinking.

"Jace, secure her apartments and when we finish here, take her there and make sure she has everything she needs. Food--clothes--necessities--"

Colton escorted Meara down the hallway, and all Jace could do was watch them walk away. His inner cat fought to get out. Hell, he needed to be with her. She was frightened and unsure. But his hopes that she would accept the position rose. He hadn't been all that sure when he'd found her huddled in the corner of her lab with sparks flying and smoke swirling. She had appeared a lost lamb, and when he'd seen her, he'd wanted to put his arms around her and reassure her. Instead he put her in cuffs.

I'm not a serial killer. He remembered her words. Little did she know she'd be working for a team who profiled mass murderers. Colton's and Meara's voices faded as they moved along the corridor.

"Hey, get your mind out of the gutter." Laughing, Hewitt slapped him on the back of his head.

"Back at ya." No, he just wanted to protect this woman and cherish her for the rest of his life. He'd never been the protective type before. But that didn't mean he didn't want to get to know her a lot better, but this time in a very different way. He grinned from the inside out and blood roared through his veins.

"Jace, I think we have a case. Northeast LA. Three victims that we know of. All women and they've been strangled then left in an old cemetery." Leia handed Jace a folder then walked to a large circular table and sat down.

Leia was what a person could call a tall blond bombshell. She did the public relations for the team, making sure all the newscasts would help them locate the unsub or unknown subject. And she also went over all of the cases, perusing them for the ones they would actually take.

He slapped the file on his leg, still staring down the hall. There was a room next to his in the complex. If he rented that one for her, would it be too obvious? Hell, everyone was already guessing at his infatuation. But it wasn't a crush. This was the real one, the forever one, he laughed inside again. He still had to convince Meara. And that might take some work. She didn't know who he really was. He would have to tell her--no show her--his secret. What a doozy it was too.

"As soon as Meara signs the contract, we will be headed to a transport," Josh said. "Relax, you'll have enough time to get her settled. Colton understands that to keep her, he's going to have to make her feel at ease. And it seems you are his ticket to relaxing the beautiful Ms. Meara. Leia left a few things for her. You can find them in that crate. Go shopping for food, just basics for now. She won't be going with us, so she will have to do her own grocery list and head for the store while we are airborne."

Hewitt was a genius, the smartest man he'd ever met. He could read a book and remember it word for word, and he spoke seven languages fluently. A bit nerdy but the nicest, most caring person he'd ever met.

"She's pretty skittish, but I suppose if I had been underground in a cubicle for almost two years, I'd be a bit shy and edgy." Jace had ideas forming in his head, and he understood better than anyone that her signing with the agency was not a given. His gut tightened at the thought of taking her to prison rather than her new home beside his. He wouldn't do it. He'd find a way to convince her to stay with him.

Jace pulled out his cell, quickly dialing the apartment manager and setting up the suite for Meara. He didn't care how transparent he was. He even had thoughts of, with owner approval, putting in a joining door. Yeah, he certainly was way too many steps ahead of their relationship.

An hour trudged by. Colton and Meara were still in the lab. He paced the corridor, every possible scenario rambling around in his head. His nerves frayed, his heart pounded and his knees threatened to

14

buckle. He wiped the sweat from his brow and pulled on his t-shirt to let in air.

When he saw Meara striding toward him, she was smiling. He breathed a sigh of relief, relaxing in the almost sure knowledge she was going to be on the team and he would learn all about Meara. His nostrils flared as he recognized her scent and the smell of her. She found him attractive. His heart melted in anticipation.

"Everything taken care of?" Colton asked.

Jace nodded. "You signing?" he asked.

"How could I not?"

He fought for control when she innocently ran her tongue over her bottom lip, leaving them wet and glistening. Hell, he wanted to taste her.

Good Lord, he'd never seen a woman so drop dead gorgeous; the way her eyes lit with a shy innocence and at the same time was so damn sexy. She had a body which made his lust burn hotter than a one hundred plus day in the Sierra Madres. He needed to wrap her in his arms and explore every inch of her sensuous body with his hands and lips.

"Be at the transport in two hours," Colton said to Jace. "Take her home first, get her settled and see that she has a way to get back here."

To Meara, "You need to be at the lab in exactly three hours."

~ * ~

Candles burned in the dimly lit room. He sat on a stool in his briefs, watching the glow of the fire and reminiscing. He couldn't forget. No matter how hard he tried, the memories reeled in his head. The humiliation and frustration he fought on a daily basis.

Painted in red on the wall was a five-pointed star. The paint had dripped and slid down the wall just as blood dripped from his victims.

He'd bound the girl's hands and feet and duck-taped her mouth. He wanted her to suffer before he killed her just as he had suffered at the hands of females for his entire life. His mother would bring men home, different men. The next day his mother would taunt him and sometimes beat him.

"Make it stop," he wailed to the empty room.

Their taunts echoed in his throbbing head. His hands pressed against his temples as if he could end the pounding. He inhaled the scent from the candles, wishing always wishing.

He rose and walked to the woman, running his hand down the column of her neck then between her breasts. It was time to find a new girl. He was tired of this one. Her hair had matted against her head and dried blood disfigured her face. Eyes once so vibrant with hatred were now dazed and unfocused.

He rolled her up in a rug and hefted her over his shoulder. A few minutes later he was in his old battered Oldsmobile, driving down River Road to the pond with the girl in the trunk.

Carefully searching the wooded area for any sign of people, he waited patiently. Then he slipped from the car, carried the girl to the pond, tossing her along with the weighted rug into the water. A shiver of pleasure traveled up his spine.

Chapter Two

"Good afternoon, Meara. Hope you are ready. No one had time to really spell out your duties because they vary from case to case," Colton told her as he packed a stack of manila envelopes filled with information into his briefcase.

"I will be ready, sir. I will find anything you need in record time." Her enthusiasm gave her pause. She was excited to do this. Gosh darn it anyway, she was no longer a hacker but a technical analyst. She liked her new title. And despite the years, the pain and the endless things that had gone wrong, she felt tears start to form in her eyes. Her parents would be pleased if they were looking down on her now. She wiped moisture from her cheek then sniffed.

"Meeting," Colton said, turning to Leia. "What do we know about the case?" His grim voice and unsmiling face resonated around the room. The atmosphere in the offices suddenly turned to tension and as appealing as spoiled food.

"Three women have been reported missing in northeast LA. They are all about five foot five, small build with red hair." She set three pictures on the desk, spreading them out as she spoke.

Meara's fingers curled on the armrests of her chair then she stiffened, gritting her teeth against what was being said, inhaling, exhaling.

"They all look the same," Jace said.

"Yes, we have a type. A fourth woman went missing an hour ago. The husband said she was at the babysitter's picking up their daughter."

"Hewitt, I want you to talk to the dad and see what he can remember. The smallest detail will help us create the profile. Take Barrister with you." Colton looked down at his cell phone then pocketed it.

"On it, Colton." The two agents picked up their gear and left.

"She must have driven off with him before the daughter could come outside," Jace said as he rubbed the back of his neck.

"McKenna, I need you to check with the locals and the police, talk to them, see if they can remember anything that will help."

"Leia, go with McKenna. Let the police know that as soon as we have a profile, we will talk to the media."

Watching the team's precision nearly took Meara's breath. She could hardly believe she was part of this, part of a team. Luck had taken her side and landed her in a safe haven. A few seconds later, she was alone. She knew she had some time before their requests would filter back to her. Memorizing her surroundings, she slowly walked to her office filled with computer screens. Her earpiece was beside the keyboard.

Meara set her cell on the desk in front of her, connecting it to her headset then settled into her chair, swirling around in circles admiring all of her new equipment. The room was lined with screens.

Her keyboard was at her fingertips. She logged in and scenes of murdered women appeared on her monitor. Horrified at what had just transpired in front of her, she hoped she could help find this fourth woman.

The rest of the team would soon be in cars on the way to the crime scene just northeast of the city. They should arrive in a couple of hours.

She brought up several maps of the area and the surrounding suburbs, locating places of interest and familiarizing herself with the terrain. Then she searched for headlines about the murders and their victims. Three of the missing women had been located, their bodies mutilated beyond recognition. Dental records and in one case fingerprints had identified the bodies. No one knew how many reported missing women were among his victims. But they all died from drowning.

Two of those women had been found washed up on the banks of a river, the third found in a small creek. It seemed the unsub had a fetish for water. Meara located several other bodies of water in the area. She felt a tremor somewhere in the pit of her belly, and for a moment she intensely hated what she was doing.

Her phone rang. "Meara, you there?"

"Sure am. What do you need, Jace?" she swallowed hard, remembering his smoldering amber eyes. She'd never thought she'd find herself so attracted to a man. Her body responded at the image in her mind and told her to flee from this predator.

"Run these names through the data base. See if you can find out anything," Jace told her, reciting the list. Jace McKenna had a scientific background and he was intuitive. Some said he was lucky, he said he went with his gut. In the beginning, he was more like the enforcer, now his intelligence was also respected.

"Got it," she said her fingers flying across the keyboard. "I'll call back as soon as I find out anything." Adrenalin pumped through her. "You, my girl, are in your element. You are doing what you love and it's legal. Amazing!"

She held a pen in one hand as she typed in the names and ran the search. As the new information popped on the screens, she jotted down notes.

"Jace, one more thing."

"I'm all ears."

"They all have arrest records. Three are in jail, but I've found a Ted Johnson who is living outside the city--2234 Toll Back Road. He recently quit his job and fell off the radar. He just didn't show up one day."

"Thanks, Meara, and keep up the good work. Look into his past and see if you can find a trigger. Something that might have happened that would have caused him to go crazy."

"You, are very welcome," she said. "Will do, and is there anything else?" Meara gritted her teeth and managed to put a tight clamp on her tangled emotions. Feelings she somehow knew would never go away. Her lower body tightened at the sound of his voice. His voice a deep sexy purr sent chills down her spine.

"See if you can trace his cell and credit cards."

"Give me one minute. Got it. Oh...oh no, he's not our man unless he can do all these things from the grave. He passed on three months ago. Died in a traffic accident on the way into the city." *Geez, girl, keep your mind on business.*

In less than twenty-four hours life had drastically changed for her. Time would tell if it was for the better. She had obligations now, people she was accountable to. Well, and if she failed...

The consequence of failure could mean life or death. Her body shuddered, thinking of Jace and the newly blossoming feelings. Emotions she had never felt before surfaced every time she looked at the dangerously macho man and his beautiful tatts. Tattoos that had drawn her to him, perhaps even called her name. Something she truly did not understand.

He was different. Something about him she couldn't quite figure out. Her mind screamed predator though. Was she his prey?

"Cell phone trace," she mumbled trying to get her mind off this man. Good Lord but he took her breath away when he looked at her and smiled that crazy lopsided grin of his. It was as if he knew what she thought, could read her mind. "Oh, I guess there's no need for that."

Meara ran her fingers over the smooth keys in front of her. She wondered what it would feel like to smooth her hands over Jace's body. She felt different sensations, things she'd never realized existed. And she felt hot from the top of her head to the tips of her toes just from thinking. The smell of his aftershave sent goose bumps down her arms too. The aroma was a little bit spicy with a tang of forest and citrus all in one.

Hours seemed to run one into another, unending as evidence gathered in front of her. Exhaustion weighed her down. How long had she been sitting here in her new office? She stared blankly at the clock-- twenty-three hours. Food and sleep were what she needed. For a few minutes she closed her eyes.

Meara rubbed the back of her neck and rolled her shoulders, trying to ease the tension gathering there. A video ran across her screen, one that made her skin crawl. "Oh, no...oh, no," She closed her eyes. Hours seemed to pass and silence filled every crevice in her head.

"Hello there, got anything new for me?" Meara could almost hear Jace's grin in the ensuing silence. She tapped her pen on the desk and cocked one eyebrow. "I'm sending video your way."

"Got it," he said then she heard. "Guys, you've got to see this."

She imagined the team surrounding Jace and their feelings when they watched what she'd just sent. The unsub had videotaped the murders and posted them on YouTube. The video had gone viral. But they now had a lead to his identity.

"What did you find out about our killer?"

"He grew up in a single parent home--living with his father. It seems his mother died of cancer when he was ten. His grades slowly fell until he ended up in Alt Ed then dropped out of school. After that he had a few odd jobs here and there, traveling around the countryside. He finally ended up in Los Angeles. He doesn't have a job but picks up a disability check every month."

"Anything on the women?"

"Tons. Julianne Anders works as a dental hygienist. She has two children and a husband of ten years. She was abducted after leaving work three months ago. She is thirty-six years old. Beth Stone was taken after someone rear-ended her car two months ago. She was thirty-two, and she had one child but she was a single parent. Her car was still idling at the stop sign. Beth was a high school art teacher. She was taken just minutes after a football game started. Evidently she'd been working at the ticket booth, but witnesses say she had to leave early to pick up another child at a friend's house. She was planning on returning to see the last of the game. Christina Vandeross was a graphic design artist. She worked for a firm here in L.A. and she was thirty-eight, no children and recently divorced. She was abducted in a parking structure. Friends say she was shopping.

"We are looking for a white male. He drives a blue van. We think his mother might have abused him. He might have a prior arrests--some of the arrests might be for animal cruelty. And her death triggered his killing."

"Good work, Meara. Josh is sending you three addresses. Triangulate and see if you can come up with a location."

"Done in nano seconds. Hold on." Meara typed in the coordinates. "Voila!" She read the information to Jace.

"Thanks, Meara."

Meara leaned back in her chair, closing her eyes. Tears for the lost women ran down her cheeks. She didn't move for the longest time. *I should go home.*

But she knew Jace would call her when they caught the man. She waited, dozed for a moment or an hour or two. She didn't look at the clock. Exhaustion swept through her. She could barely keep her eyelids up. She felt hot and sweaty. Good Lord, but she needed a shower.

Finally, her cell rang. She hesitated before picking up. "Hi. You caught the killer?"

"Not yet. He left before we could get there. The police chief leaked information to the press."

"What can I do?" she asked.

"I'm going to need your help. Run electricians who drive blue Ford vans. Jace's voice was grim.

"On it. I'll have everything you need ASAP."

Meara hung up and began the process. Her fingers danced over the keyboard, bringing up DMV records as well as work history on anyone fitting the description. The emptiness vanished as she put her mind to work. But thoughts of Jace grew stronger. Just thinking about him made her palms sweat and her pulse race.

"Damn," she muttered, continuing to find information that shed no new light on the location of the killer.

She sat back, closing her eyes, taking in all of the sounds surrounding her and trying to think of something different. Her stomach growled. She was used to hunger, but sleeplessness was a different commodity. Finally, she rose and wandered down the hallway to the vending machines. She pushed a dollar bill through the slot and poked the button for a cup of coffee. Repeating this, she bought a bag of chips and a fiber bar. "Yum," she muttered sarcastically. Then she walked back to her office.

"Oh my!" She raked her hands through her hair. They are coming home just in time. She leaned in closer to the monitor as if that would clarify what she saw. The description of the girl and the location were very similar. It seemed the killer had come home to them--to the city.

Was it a taunt? Shivers spiraled up her back and arms. She stood and paced, watching the surrounding monitors. Cringing inside and wondering if she could do this, really do this. The images were so horrible.

How could the team keep coming back to this?

She'd only been part of this team for a little over a day, and the sights she'd seen were horrifying. Death was never a pleasant thought, but what she'd seen was torture and rape. She continued working. The afternoon sunshine faded to darkness and the room took on an eerie color from the screen lights.

"How you doing?"

She jumped, her hand racing to her chest to stop the sudden pounding of her heart. "Oh my, Oh, my, you scared me." When she worked, she tuned everything out. Actually, she was surprised she heard his question, but she'd sensed him there less than a second before the words were uttered.

Jace stood in the doorway, feet apart, hands at his sides. He cocked his head slightly as he watched her. "I'm sorry, didn't mean to frighten you. What have you got there?" He stepped closer then peered over her shoulder at the screen.

"I have seen terrible things, things I wouldn't wish on my worst enemy. I don't want to feel but..." Tears that had been held back all day suddenly slipped from her eyes. With the back of her hand, she wiped them away.

He was beside her then, and in a brotherly fashion pulling her into his arms, warmth surrounding her. Meara rested her head on his chest and closed her eyes, reveling in a security she hadn't felt in such a long time. His muscles, even in stillness seemed to ripple and move with a steadiness she didn't understand. "We still have a lot of work to do." For a moment he held her at arms distance as he stared into her eyes.

She'd never been held by a man, not like this. Her father had often wrapped his arms around her, but he was her father.

"Have you been home?"

"No, I..."

"You haven't slept in over twenty-four hours. I'll take you there."

"Sleep is overrated and you haven't slept either. I don't think either one of us is going home anytime soon." Fervently, she wished she could go home and sleep for the next twelve hours.

"Nope, we are going home now, this very minute. Sometimes sleep gives us a new perspective on things. Colton will call if anything happens. We're working in shifts until we figure out who this guy is or catch up at least halfway on our sleep."

"Is that what you are hoping for? A new assessment?"

His laughter rumbled in his chest. She smiled, hearing his heart beat next to her face, his scent and his warmth filling her soul. Once again the emptiness that had encompassed her for so very long seemed to vanish.

He turned her and draped an arm over her shoulder then led her from the building and to his car. She settled into the seat and listened to the roar of the car. The sun was just dipping behind the buildings, and the sky was mottled with beautiful colors. The scent of daphnia hung on the air.

"Hope you like your new apartment. We are in the same building. There is a large park nearby with a river running through it. The beach is close and the Pacific Ocean is gorgeous most days. You will be able to watch the sun set every evening if you want. Or at least evenings you are not working.

An hour or so later they pulled to a stop in front of a Spanish style building. White stucco with a brilliant red roof stood out against the brilliance of the blue sky and the colors of the setting sun.

"Here we are, Meara," Jace said as he ushered her inside the building and up the steps to the two side-by-side apartments.

"One of these is yours, isn't it?" Meara asked, cocking her head slightly and liking the feelings emanating from Jace. She felt protected and secure. The realization sent a warm fuzzy feeling radiating inside out.

"Do you mind?" He turned her so they were looking at each other as if he wanted to see into her soul.

"No," Meara touched his lips with her index finger and reveled in the shiver that seemed to sweep through him. She had never felt this kind of power or even tested her powers of seduction before. The urge had never been present before Jace McKenna appeared out of nowhere to rock her world with seismic ferocity. She certainly wasn't innocent, but she also had never understood that pure lust could take over her entire being, and that she couldn't stop thinking about this man.

"Good, I'm glad you like it. I'll let you settle in, but I'll be back in about two hours, and I will fix you dinner," Jace said.

"I'll bring the wine." Cocking her head to the side, she focused on the man. "What will you be doing for the next two hours?"

26

"I am going for a run in the hills behind us."

"Oh..."

Running was not one of her favorite pursuits. Meara didn't mind a leisurely walk along the beach or on an easy hiking trail, but running...

"I'm not asking you to share all of my interests. At least not yet," he said and tapped her on the nose.

"I'm kind of the geeky sort." Her voice barely worked. His touches were sending her over the top. She clenched her hands to keep from shaking, at the same time trying not to give her emotions away as her clit pulsed and her panties grew damp.

"Dear lady, you are anything but geeky. You are drop dead gorgeous." He stepped back, crossing his arms over his chest and slanted her what she could only describe as a devilish look.

"Then I will see you later." Meara stepped inside, and closing the door behind her, she leaned against it and gazed at the living room. Her place! This was her very own real first home. After she'd run from her parent's death, she'd found her escape in the underground. She lived from hour to hour and day to day. Never knowing if she would have food to eat or if she'd go hungry.

First thing, Meara strode to the balcony. Stepping out onto it she rested her hands on the railing and gazed out at the huge Pacific Ocean. Salt air filled her senses, and a tiny breeze stirred the leaves of a nearby tree. How had her luck changed so dramatically in a matter of a couple of days? A strange giddiness enveloped her, and she was struck with the mood to dance.

Wandering into her apartment, she rambled from room to room. The kitchen wasn't spacious, but the countertops and appliances were adequate for her needs. Once she had enjoyed baking. She'd never really learned to cook. But that was what recipes were for. Experimenting could be fun.

In the bedroom closet she pulled out several dresses, tops and pants. Had Jace picked these out for her while she was learning the ins and outs of her brand new computer lab? If so, she liked his taste. Holding a dark blue dress with a small floral print to her face, she inhaled the scent of new clothing. She held it close to her body then danced through the room to the bathroom where she could look at herself in the mirror.

Looking good, girlfriend.

She made a mental note to thank Jace McKenna for everything he had done for her. Her entire apartment was furnished. She had clothes in her closet and food in her fridge. Pinching herself, just to make sure she wasn't dreaming, she plopped down on the sofa and picked up an electronic reader sitting on the end table then put it back. She didn't feel like reading.

She wanted Jace back from his run. She needed to look into his eyes. She wanted to know if the hunger she'd seen in them before was still there.

She wanted Jace to kiss her. The man was gorgeous. No doubt he could have any woman he wanted. She wanted to revel in his fragrance, tear off his clothes and explore every rippling muscle of his sleek body.

Trying to shake off her crazy imagination and the pooling sexual tension, Meara walked to the bathroom, determined to take a long soak in a bubble bath. She found the bath salts and poured herself a glass of wine. When she was ensconced in the tub, she took a long swallow of the merlot. It was therapeutic. It warmed her to her toes. It warmed away some of the tension deep inside. But it did nothing to take her mind from Jace. If anything, the alcohol accentuated every thought and emotion.

She leaned back and closed her eyes. Her heart was thundering. Close your eyes, she told herself. Relax. She had to relax, but when she closed her eyes, the pictures of the poor women on the videos turned to nightmares. Jace had somehow taken a second seat to the investigation.

She opened her eyes and pushed away the pictures in her mind, replacing them with images of Jace. The hot steam of the bath rose around her, and she felt her tension begin to ease. She took another long sip of her wine then closed her eyes and leaned her head against the rim of the tub.

Meara sighed softly then opened her lashes. Darkness was falling rapidly. Jace would soon return from his run and they would have dinner. She rose from the tub, wrapping a towel around her before passing the medicine cabinet mirror.

She paused and smoothed her hair back. She was still staring at herself a second later, she realized. She was wondering if Jace found her attractive. The years underground had in ways aged her. The color of her hair would have to be changed, she decided. She couldn't go around now that she was in the bureau with all the decorative colors in it.

Standing away from the mirror slightly, she looked at her blond, blond roots. She was a natural blond. As a teenager she'd had white blond hair that had hung nearly to her waist. Now her hair was ragged and layered, and she hadn't had a decent cut in she didn't know how many years. She had huge blue eyes, and she was horrifyingly skinny with few curves. But try as she might, she couldn't gain weight. She hated being skinny and knowing that others never empathized.

Walking into the bedroom and standing in front of the closet, she chose a simple blue summer dress to wear, hoping it would make her eyes pop. She started down the hallway and across the living room. It was only when she was halfway to the kitchen that she realized she'd left the television on, and that the newscast was about the case they were investigating.

"--and it is believed at this time the serial killer has struck again. The body of another young woman was pulled from Lake..."

Meara plopped down on the couch, her face on her hands. Tears flowed freely for the woman she didn't know--another woman she could not save.

~ * ~

The man stood outside her apartment, staring at her open balcony door. The breeze off the ocean ruffled his hair. Absentmindedly, he pushed a stray lock from his face. His heart beat a rapid staccato beneath his ribs as he felt the ever-present surge of need.

Meara opened the doors and stood in silhouette for a few strained moments as the man felt all of his senses kick to life. He was sure he could smell the soft scent of lemon drift toward him from the heights above.

He gritted his teeth, knowing he must wait. He couldn't have her now. Her friend, Jace McKenna, was too close. "Too close," he muttered. "Too close."

The doors opened and she walked onto the porch, bracing her hands on the railing, tilting her head upward. He watched the breeze grab hold of her hair and toss it around her face. She let go of the balustrade to pull it back and hold it behind her head. When she turned, he caught site of her from the side.

To him, she was breathtaking. But he would change her clothes. Her skirt was too short, too provocative. She would wear things like this for him only. No one else would see her this undressed.

30

A long low growl caught in his throat, and he sensed a presence behind him, walking toward the apartments. He blended into the shadows of the rocks lining the pathway to the beach and watched.

Jace McKenna sauntered cat-like along the path. Arrogant man-- didn't anything faze him? His muscles bulged and rippled as he walked. The rosettes looked like dirt on his darkly tanned body. When he had Meara, the first thing he would do is get rid of her tatts. He hated them.

He'd watched Meara walk arm in arm with Jace from the bureau building a couple of hours ago, and he'd known the minute she'd run her bath and settled into the warmth. He massaged the muscles in the back of his neck.

He hunkered down and watched for a few more minutes then turned and left, mapping out his plan for Meara's abduction.

Chapter Three

The park was thick with trees and miles long, stretching into the hills. Jace loved to come here. When he was far enough away and off the hiking trails, he could shed his skin and change his form. Then he could run. Outside his human shape he felt free--all his senses heightened.

He could barely contain his excitement. The tension that came with his job could be unbearable at times. He often wondered how the other members of his team coped with the stress. Perhaps they were also shapeshifters. The thought made him grin and sent crazy shivers down his spine. Of course he had never told anyone about his abilities. No one would believe him. And no one would no how to profile him.

He jogged a few miles farther into the hills. Shielding himself with a tree for camouflage, he disrobed then hid his clothes behind a huge boulder. He felt his calf muscles begin to tingle with the increased blood flow, felt the sensation inch up his body, experienced the increase of adrenalin surge through his prepared body. He had just shifted into his cat form--a sleek black jaguar. Even in his human form, his cat never left him. It was always there prowling around in his head.

Suddenly he was on all fours and racing through the underbrush. Brambles tore at his coat and scratched his face, but he exhilarated in the run and all of the sensations revolving around him. He felt one with the world and sometimes he didn't want to return to humanity.

Unable to keep the vigorous pace for very long, he was more the zero to sixty in three minutes type, he slowed to a moderate walking pace, continuing through the forested hills and higher into the unexplored mountain range. Taking in all of the sights, smells and sounds of the area.

He knew the hills were dotted with a few homes, and he had scented man a few times, but so far he had never seen people. He was just too far away from civilization. A fire scarred area appeared to his left so he zigged right, disliking the scent of the charred trees and bushes.

The aroma of water filled his nostrils. He turned right once more, walking perpendicular to the fire scorched area. A few moments later, he crested a hill and looked upon a small lake. Scurrying down the embankment, he jumped into the water and swam. Dipping his head, filling his mouth with the taste of the liquid, he enjoyed everything about the water sweeping across his body.

Thoughts of Meara flowed through his head. What would she think of him if she knew? Did she enjoy swimming as much as he did or even a little? Would she run from him if she knew what he was? He'd never told anyone about his shifting, never trusted anyone enough, not even his friends at the bureau. Yet when he'd been at home in Sierra Madre Mountains, he'd heard stories about the love between mates. He'd never believed those tales would come true for him. But now...

Well, he'd not been prepared for the strange penetrating experience of realizing Meara was his. He needed her more than life itself, and she called to him every moment whether she was by his side or miles away.

He reached the other side and decided to hunt. He needed more food than a small barbecued steak. Making a pig of himself with their first shared meal was not part of his plan for wooing Meara. Lifting his head, he inhaled a deep breath of the wind. His tail twitched and his claws expanded.

Fox.

His stomach growled. Time was of the essence. Swooping in for the kill, he caught his prey and devoured the small animal quickly. Dusk had come and gone. Stars were twinkling in the darkening sky, and he hoped he wouldn't find Meara asleep when he returned.

A full moon shone brightly in the night sky. When he pushed open Meara's door and called out to introduce himself, he heard slightly off-key humming. A tiny shiver of apprehension swept through him. The scent of lemon stirred him and sent blood rushing within.

"Anyone home?"

"Just uncorked the wine. Well, the second bottle. Want a glass?" Meara's voice soothed him and touched a part deep inside. It sounded like summer sunlight and reminded him of a soft breeze.

He wanted to snuggle in close and purr. Damn but he didn't need to scare her. He stiffened his spine and squared his shoulders, inhaled deeply, one more time then continued into the kitchen.

"Love one, beautiful." He set the wrapped steaks on her counter then walked onto the balcony to rev up the barbecue.

"Here you go, handsome," she shot back at him.

"Thanks." He swirled the wine in the glass then smelled the heady aroma before he tasted. "Hmm..."

He could never get over just how beautiful she was. Meara ignited a spark inside him no one else had ever been able to do. And he hoped and prayed they were in a similar place where their lives were concerned. She looked like a beautiful princess with her startling blue, almost cobalt, eyes and, well, her silky hair was a crazy array of colors defining her personality. Her features were near perfect. Her face was oval, her cheekbones defined, her lips generous but beautifully shaped, and her eyebrows with a little arch that could give her an all-knowing look of extreme intelligence. She was one of a kind, and she wore her personality well.

Jace had been born to shapeshifter parents. His mother Native American, Apache, and his father was white Anglo Saxon--Scottish. His village was in the Sierra Madre Mountains in Mexico and isolated-- far away from everything modern and everyone who could harm them. Running wild as he grew, he experienced the country and the dry desert plateaus of the area. He loved the sparse vegetation, tumble weeds, and the cactus made everything seem clean.

Joining the bureau had always been a dream of his, and it was perhaps made easier by the fact that he had Apache blood. He was a minority and they had to consider him--place him at the top of the line. But only his expertise had secured his job with the profiling team. The jaguar was known as the God of the Night and was formidable lord of the underworld. His name meant moon. Was he a child of the moon?

Perhaps in his line of work there was more truth to this than he wanted to believe. After all, he put away serial killers and fought the wicked. He encountered unimaginable and unbelievable maliciousness almost everyday of his life. If he didn't see the cruelty with his own eyes, he wouldn't believe some of the maliciousness existed.

They would be on the job again tomorrow, and he wondered why the killer from the outskirts of Los Angelis had left his signature in LA. For what reason had he come to their home? He had moved out of his comfort zone, changing his profile. And that fact was highly unusual for a serial killer.

"A penny for your thoughts?"

"Oh, I don't think they are worth a penny. But I was thinking about my younger years, my home."

"Are your parents alive?" She sipped her wine all the while staring at him with a lopsided grin that sent his sexual fantasy into second gear.

"Yes, I don't get to see them very much though. Work and all." Jace made a conscious effort to look into Meara's eyes, gorgeous eyes. Learning about Meara, inside and out, the most imperative item on his agenda.

"I miss mine, my parents." She cocked her head inquisitively to the side. She looked sad and suddenly withdrawn. He wanted to wrap his arms around her and tell her everything would be fine.

But he couldn't, not right now. He had to find out more about this woman, his mate.

"I'm sorry. Tell me about them." He placed the steaks on the grill then turned toward her, wishing he could see inside her head, perhaps heal all of her wounds. Perhaps in time she would give him the opportunity to help.

"They were so smart and loving," she said. "They put me first, would do anything for me." She ran her finger around the rim of her glass, seeming to watch the red liquid swirl and dance inside. She closed her eyes and he wanted to be inside her head, needed to know what she wasn't telling him.

He had his demons, demons he'd never spoke of to anyone. It had taken him a long time to become comfortable in both of his worlds. When he moved to the states he'd had to be so very careful. No one here understood that a man could shift into another form. At times he'd felt as if he had some incurable defect that he was somehow damaged. In time he embraced the beauty of his heritage. But most people, if they knew who he really was, would consider him defective and his shapeshifting a disability. They would brand him as an undesirable and probably cross to the other side of the street when they walked past him.

"What kind of animals do you like?" The question came out of the blue, but he was glad he asked. Maybe she would say jaguar was her favorite. Maybe not. Perhaps he should just blurt out what he was. He swallowed hard, tamping down his impatience. The last thing he wanted was to scare her.

"I've never really thought about it," she said cocking her head to the side as if thinking. She sipped her wine again. "I like all animals. I am most assuredly an animal lover and activist."

Well, that was an encouraging start. "What is your favorite? Everyone has to have a favorite. It's kind of like colors. We all have a favorite color and a favorite food, even a favorite time of day."

She closed her eyes then her lids flipped open. She was staring at him as if she could see through him, as if she knew. "I love big cats. When I go to the zoo, I always go there first. Lions and tigers--the cheetahs are so gorgeous with their rosettes."

"What about the black ones?" Suddenly tense, he waited, anticipating what he wanted to hear. Beneath his jeans his cock hardened. He clenched his fist in an effort for control. She gazed at him and he could see a gorgeous brew of amazement and hunger churning in her beautiful blue eyes.

"Oh, I think they have rosettes too." She smiled cat-like at him, almost as if she knew where the cream was. Then she licked her lips.

Dear God, save me from myself. "They do," he said on a soft sigh, his heart pounding beneath his ribs. "You just can't see them as easily but they are there." He had the urge to show her all of his rosettes, but knew she would probably be shocked to tears if he suddenly disrobed.

He put the finished steaks on the plates. She dished up the salad and roasted zucchini. They ate in silence. He relished the taste of the meat much more than the vegetables. He noticed she didn't finish her steak but ate all of the zucchini and had seconds on the salad. At least with food, they were total opposites.

"The jaguar's rosettes were my inspiration."

"Your tattoo?" The thought she liked the big cat's markings enough to put one on her body inspired and sent a thrill down his spine. He heard the flash of blood, felt the rapid beat of his heart. Yet, he knew he shouldn't rush her with the knowledge. Shapeshifting was far different from a permanent drawing on ones body. His cat prowled through his head, begging for release.

She yawned then covered her mouth with her hand. He eyed the steak she'd left thinking about eating the food.

"I do believe I'm exhausted. I'll clean this up in the morning." She finished her glass of wine.

This was his invitation to exit. A run on the beach would be wonderful. Waiting until after midnight imperative. He had a place to run where there were rocks nearby just in case another person invaded his space or he could run in his human form.

"I'll do the dishes," he told her, "then I'm going down to the beach. I'll take you to work tomorrow."

"You sure?"

"Positive, now go." He smiled when she turned and hugged him. She felt so damn good. This evening had gone well. He meant to take it one step further. Tonight or tomorrow he wasn't sure. But she liked cats and he wondered how she would react to seeing a black jaguar in her bedroom. A shiver of excitement swept through him. The scent of her, of lemon, lingered on the air. As he finished the dishes, he ate the remaining meat before sauntering outside to run once more.

He had a plan.

But was it a good plan? Should he question her more? Was it too much too soon? He didn't like the insecurity and second-guessing himself.

On the beach he hid his clothes in a protected spot then shifted. Once again the adrenalin flowed from his feet to his head. He let out a low growl when he started to run. He sprinted close to the rocks, but there was no one to hide from. Running for about five minutes, he moved closer to the breaking waves then into the water. Sea spray from his paws pounding the water, hit his face then he lapped at the water. Salt stung his nostrils and the moon hovered in the black velvet sky.

When he was exhausted, he shifted back and dressed in the white-t and jeans he left at the rocks. Staring up at her apartment he inhaled a long deep breath, his mind suddenly clear. In a few moments he was in his apartment. Shifting back to his cat form, he leapt from his balcony to hers.

~ * ~

Meara snuggled in closer to the furry warmth next to her. "Hmm..." She purred as she stroked the soft fur. She knew she didn't want this dream to end, but she understood it would. She kept her eyes closed and tried to memorize the sensations. A few moments later she woke again with a tickle in her ear. She brushed her ear and felt soft hair against her hand. Her body thrummed to life, her blood rushing through her at an incredible pace. She didn't want to open her eyes and encounter daylight just yet. Lying in this dream was such an incredible experience.

"Not time to get up," she mumbled, her body slow to respond to the daylight but not to the form next to hers. Her heart pounded, her clit pulsed and she moaned low in her throat, arching tightly.

A very soft warm growl filled her with a sense of protection. All of her defenses were down and she suddenly did not feel alone. She had been dependent on herself for so long she liked this feeling, didn't want to loose it. Afraid if she opened her eyes this wonderful sensation would vanish. She had always wanted someone to protect her. Meara's thoughts jumped to Jace.

"Jace..."

He would be at her door soon. Like a lightening bolt, a surge of early morning adrenalin shot through her. She needed to get up and take a shower and she wanted to eat breakfast. She was hopeless without her morning meal. Opening her eyes she looked into a pair of big green cat eyes.

"Yikes! Oh my god."

Terrified energy pumped through her body and her heart pounded in her throat as she jumped out of the bed and onto the floor. Knees quivering, she froze to the spot. Yet knowing she needed to regain her senses, she tried to think of something to do that would get her out of her bedroom unscathed.

"Go away..." Holding her hands out in front of her as if that gesture would do her any good if he decided to eat her, she watched the cat rise from the covers, stretch languidly then leap from the bed as if he was accustomed to sleeping on her bed--as if he owned her bed. They stood on opposite sides of the mattress staring at each other. The cat shook his head as if he was saying, *I'm going to be here every night. What are you going to do about it?* The cat's tail twitched rhythmically back and forth then up and down.

Before she could scream--well, she wasn't sure she should yell-- as if he were king, the cat cocked his head to the side and with a swish of his tail strode from her room. She couldn't help herself. She followed and watched the cat saunter onto her balcony and gracefully leap to Jace's balcony. Her body froze then she unpeeled the ice from around her rigid limbs and ran for her door.

I've got to warn him!

What if the cat kills him? He didn't kill me. He seemed to really like me...and he seemed very cocky and a little bit arrogant and acted as if he owned me. *The cat kind of sort of reminds me of someone.*

She rushed to the outside door and realized she was dressed in a skimpy negligee that was at the moment falling from her shoulders. "Oh my, oh my, oh..." This could be a matter of life and death. She inhaled and exhaled, wiped the sweat from her brow then stiffened her spine. Warning Jace was imperative, but she was terrified.

The coat stand held a longish sweater. Donning it quickly, she rushed from her apartment to Jace's.

"Jace, Jace, are you awake? Open up! Please..." she pounded on the door. "Jace, you've got to..."

Fully clothed, he opened the door. "There is a huge b-black c-cat--" Her arms whirled awkwardly in big circles, trying to show him just how big and black and monstrous and vicious the cat was. But he wasn't vicious. That wasn't fair.

One elegant eyebrow rose. "A black cat? Vicious?" His voice was husky and low. It was sexy and sensual and deeply masculine and the sound touched her as no other ever had. He was grinning from ear to ear, staring at her as if she were half crazy. "You don't say."

"I saw, he jumped from my balcony to yours." Her speech slowed and for a moment her breath caught as she poked her head around him to see in the room. "I'm hallucinating." She inhaled a swift deep breath, hoping to calm her nerves.

"I'm sure you just had a dream. There is no huge black cat here." His grin seemed to stretch from ear to ear.

"A nightmare, no it wasn't a nightmare. It was..." She was suddenly aware of more hot sensations, wonderful sensations, intense sensations. Her body thrummed to life sending her sexual fantasies. "I needed to warn you."

"Meara? Were you afraid? Why didn't you scream for me?"

"I couldn't say anything. No, I was afraid at first. Who wouldn't be if they woke up and a huge black jaguar was lying next to you in your bed licking your ear. Oh, my god, I am hallucinating."

"Licking your ear, you say."

"Well no, I don't know if he licked my ear." She touched her ear. "I thought he did, but now I'm not sure of anything."

Jace put his arm around her and pulled her close. She let him hold her and imagined Jace licking her ear. She loved his scent. Pushing away from him, she looked into a pair of eyes that were strikingly similar to the cat's eyes.

I am going certifiably insane.

"I'll fix breakfast. You go do whatever girls do. Eggs, bacon and toast will be ready when you are." He paused for a moment, smile still firmly in place, but this time the grin looked a lot wicked. "I'd like to lick your ear and other parts," he said with a low growl that also sounded strangely familiar.

"No, no, no, I'm not crazy. I just worked too hard yesterday and the day before. No food, no sleep, just computers humming in front of me. And horrid pictures filling the screens." She paced back and forth inside his living room then stopped.

"Everything okay?"

"Hmmm... maybe I'll give you the chance," she winked then slipped back to her apartment door, feeling the heat of embarrassment as well as sexual arousal on her cheeks. All he had to do was look at her. She turned to gaze at him one more time. She was standing there with her wispy negligee and a barely there sweater, wondering how she could have imagined something so ridiculous.

Watching her he laughed, clearly amused, and slowly his lips curled in the way she was beginning to recognize as pure Jace then he slanted her an easy sensual smile like the one he'd given her last night. It was one that had sent her body into overdrive. She felt the same response right now. Her nipples hardened painfully, begging to be explored and tasted by Jace.

She longed to move into his arms and forget all about work, even though she loved her job--well parts of her job--catching the bad guy part. He seemed to carry an unearthly strength, and she was suddenly quite certain his air of total confidence had not come to him without just cause. He was a powerful man; she could feel it in the vibrant heat that seemed to enclose him.

Something warm seemed to sizzle through her and around her-- between them. Once again her heart began to thunder.

"Aren't you supposed to be fixing breakfast? I like my eggs scrambled, Mister McKenna, sir," she said, slipping through the door to the inside of her apartment. For long seconds, she leaned against the door with her eyes shut, listening to the pounding of her heart and the roar of the waves against the sand, or was it the roar the blood rushing through her veins.

Racing through the living room to the shower, she tore off the sweater and her tattered nightgown, wondering what on earth had happened to it. Maybe she wasn't certifiably insane, or had she done this herself? Ripped her clothes? Then she realized for the first time in more years than she could remember, her sleep had not been filled with nightmares.

"Geez, girl," she muttered. "What have you been on?" She had done her share of drugs, but that was in her past. She'd been clean for the last year. And--she had never experienced anything like last night. What she remembered felt so real it could not be a fantasy.

A black jaguar in my room, in my bed, purring softly next to me. Had it really cuddled next to her all night long?

The hot shower water washed over her in a steady stream. Hurrying with her hair and shaving her legs, she was out in less than ten minutes. She made a mental note to search her computers for facts about the big cat she'd imagined last night as well as search the area for any escapees from zoos.

She just couldn't quite wrap her mind around the fact that she might have imagined the incident. After quickly dressing, she rushed back to Jace's apartment to be greeted with the wonderful smells of bacon and eggs emanating from the front door. This time she didn't knock but walked into the room, announcing herself.

"Jace, I'm here."

"Come on into the kitchen, baby girl," he called out, making her smile at the sound of his low husky voice. Meara wanted to bring up the topic of the cat, but then she didn't want to either. Jace seemed so nonchalant about her early morning hysteria almost as if he knew something he didn't want to tell.

"I'm famished." She sat down at the table where a huge plate of food was set. Picking up a fork, she waved it in the air, gesturing to him. "Are you sure you didn't see a big black cat this morning?"

"Positive, but I might have seen a little black cat."

She was still waving the fork at him. "You are incorrigible." His gentle teasing sent a flutter of goose bumps down her arms.

"You think I'm hopeless?" He dug into his plate of food.

She smiled slowly, enjoying the moment and the casual play on words. "You know what I mean. And I know what I saw. I'm not going to let myself think I'm crazy." She sat back in her chair, cocking her head, studying him then listening to the sounds of the ocean and wondering what the future might bring.

He leaned forward, resting his forearms on the table, still smiling. "I don't think you are crazy. I've heard rumors that there have been sightings of a black jaguar roaming the hills. But to end up in your bedroom and in your bed--that gives a man a reason to pause and think."

"Are you safe when you run in those hills?" A sudden jolt of fear pummeled through her. She rubbed her arms to stop the chill.

He exhaled on a very long sigh then turned his head away. She didn't like what she saw in his eyes. He was lying to her, she was sure. Then his expression changed. His eyes were focused on her mouth. He rose, walking seductively to her chair and pulled her into his arms. Then he wasn't touching her at all, but she felt the warmth that radiated from him as if it was the glow of a fire enveloping her.

"I was just wondering if I had to compete against this cat that snuggled with you in your bed last night," he said while he traced her earlobe with one fingertip.

She didn't have time to respond before his head lowered and his mouth caught hold of her, and waves of sensation flooded throughout her limbs and her torso and rushed wickedly along the length of her spine. His tongue flicked softly over her lips and gained entrance. She should have made this harder for him, but she couldn't find the strength within her. Her parents had always told her to resist a man's seductive ploys. She trembled, wishing it didn't feel so darn good, wishing she wasn't still thinking about that damn black cat. Wishing the mere contact with Jace's mouth didn't cause such an explosion of passion and desire.

He stepped back, staring at her with such a very intense gaze. If she hadn't caught herself instantly, she would have fallen. Her eyes lids flew open, and she could still feel his mouth touching hers. She touched a trembling finger to her lips. Body quivering, she tried to step away both physically and emotionally.

She couldn't.

One eyebrow cocked upward in a somewhat mocking gesture. "Am I safe in the hills? Probably. I think one look at me and the cat would turn tale and run in the opposite direction."

"Are you telling me the truth?" The question seemed to hang in the air wanting and needing a response that wasn't forthcoming.

His cell buzzed in his pocket. "Okay, yeah, we're on our way." He slanted her a frown and nodded to the door.

"That was Colton. He's calling us all in. He thinks that last night we were on to something."

"Saved by the cell phone," she muttered under her breath not expecting Jace to hear her.

"What was that?"

"Nothing."

"Need to go back to your apartment?"

"No." *Who are you really, Jace McKenna and what are you not telling me?*

Chapter Four

As if he felt the hair on the back of his neck stiffen, Jace froze for a moment, appearing to Meara that every animal instinct had just kicked in. His fingers around her elbow tightened.

"What's wrong?" she asked, watching his ever-changing features. And those eyes, the way they seemed to deepen in color, almost as if he were hunting. She wondered at his prey as she rubbed her hands up and down her arms.

Jace looked over his shoulder then picked up their pace. "I believe someone is following us."

"I feel it too," she said. "I feel as if someone's eyes are boring into my back. It gives me the creepy crawlies."

Moving in close, a wicked grin on his lips and leaning in low to meet her eyes, he whispered, "Stick with me, baby girl. It's probably just the huge black cat, looking for an easy meal." His smile deepened.

A shiver of warmth snaked the length of her spine, and for a moment she could barely breathe. She wanted to be alone with him, discover what made him who he was. But she was afraid too. "That wasn't very nice. Just because you didn't see the animal, doesn't mean he wasn't there." She tried for a note of indignation but failed miserably.

"Hmm," he murmured, "Maybe I should stay in your room every night to protect you from the black jag."

Sexual awareness between them was just too potent. She stifled a shiver, wishing for just what he said. Trying to ignore a verbal response to his suggestion, "I'm going to check out the local zoos and see if there were any circuses around that might have lost a jaguar."

"You do that. I'd like to know if I need to be extra careful on my runs." He surprised her with a sexy wink and a devilish grin.

The way he looked at her brought every sense alive and throbbing. It was almost as if they were reliving that first kiss. His kiss, his touch, so evocative and mercuric.

They barely knew each other, yet it seemed they had been together for a lifetime. And she knew she wanted to find out what made Jace McKenna click.

"Meara!"

It seemed she jumped a mile at the sound of his voice. She spun towards him. They were at the black SUV, his fingers circling the handle, ready, his gaze razor sharp, his voice commanding.

She could hold her own.

She smiled sweetly at him. She just had to remember he liked to tease, that was all. Then she'd be just fine.

"Let's go," he said.

She circled around him and settled into the passenger seat, riding shotgun, her smile in place. Her thoughts focused on the case.

"You're right. We're needed."

She was trembling inside, and all of her old insecurities seemed to surface in the cool morning air.

The sun was bright, warming the earth, sending heat waves shimmering off the street. It would be a scorcher today. There were few cars on the road as they approached the city and bureau office. Jace led the way through the parking lot and up the stairs.

"Do we always work on Saturday?" Meara paused, arching a brow then decided it was probably a stupid question. "Never mind."

"Yeah, well, we work whenever there is a case. And that is most of the time. We have been known to get a day off here and there."

When they walked through the halls and into the main offices, the rest of the team was already assembled, discussing the unsub and trying to look at the case in a new light. Meara sat down in an office chair near the back of the room. She wasn't really needed for any of this. She wasn't a profiler. She watched and listened, wondering what her role would be and what they would ask of her.

The team finally left and she walked into the computer lab, sitting down then logging into the terminals. She was alone, totally alone. She used to like the feeling. But now she just felt kind of empty. Moisture started to fill her eyes. Wiping them away she looked through blurry eyes at the monitor.

"You are really acting stupid, you know."

She left her station and hurried to the restroom. Splashing water on her face, she decided she felt a little bit better but she was sure her eyes would be puffy and red. It didn't take much. And she didn't understand why the memories started exploding in her mind. She'd lost so very much in her short life. And she didn't want to care about anyone, particularly anyone who could die.

She clenched her teeth hard to hold the emotions surging inside her at bay. She didn't want to remember, she hated remembering. Maybe it had all started with the crazy black cat and maybe with Jace's nonchalance when it came to his job and running in the hills where a big black jaguar could so easily end his days. But this job, the tension and finding people to care about brought memories of her past rushing over her.

Julianne had been so little and her name so big. Just three months old. And her parents had tried for so long to have another child. Her mom had become concerned, her dad telling her that trying was the most fun in the whole world. At the time she didn't quite understand what he meant. And she vividly remembered the day her mom told her she was going to have a brother or sister. When her parents brought the baby home from the hospital, she knew Julianne was the most beautiful little girl in the world. With huge blue eyes and barely any hair--so light that what there was of it you couldn't even see it, and she had adored her.

But then one night everything changed. She heard her mother screaming and woke up from a wonderful dream. She'd run into the baby's room and saw her dad bent over the baby, trying to give it mouth-to-mouth resuscitation. Her mom was dialing 911. He didn't quit until the paramedics arrived.

There was nothing anyone could do. It was sudden infant death syndrome, the doctor explained, so tragic, a horrible loss, and only God could understand. And she had cried and cried and hated God with all her might. Her dad had been the rock of the family, holding it all together, until he too died in the hateful car accident.

It was just a little later that she lost herself. She started doing weird things like chalking her hair purple and donning black lipstick. She began to lash out at everyone and everything. Maybe it was her way of trying to crawl out of the lonely well of pain encompassing her. Maybe she had wanted to fight because fighting made her feel as if they were still alive. It made her feel as if she were alive. She fought as only she knew how, teaching herself code so she could hack into places that weren't fit for human kind. But as the years passed, she withdrew even farther into herself.

"God doesn't exist," she mumbled to herself. "If there was a God, he wouldn't let psychopaths live in this world."

But then the phone rang and she heard Jace's voice in her ear. Good she had work to do and things to look up. She could stop wallowing in self-pity and thinking about non-existent gods.

Jace ran off a long list of things for her to do and find. She signed off and let her fingers and her brain take over. Work soothed her soul when she didn't want to think about her past only the present and perhaps a future.

An hour later she sent the info back to the team, waiting for anything new. She didn't want to be in the field, but she hated not knowing what was happening. An instant bond had formed between her and the team. They were like her babies and she loved them.

She didn't hear from them again. Hours passed and nothing buzzed through her phone lines. She was becoming a bit claustrophobic. She needed to escape the close confines of her lab. She didn't want to know that someone else had to die for the team to find the killer.

And she didn't want to be alone. She wanted Jace so badly. But she didn't know if he even cared that way for her. He'd been funny and teasing, but she didn't want to fall in love.

She refused to fall in love.

She just wanted someone to be there for her, wanted to be held in his arms, wanted his kiss, wanted his naked body next to hers, wanted to make love to him. Needed hot, all-consuming sex.

Suddenly Colton was on the line, rattling off more instructions. Keeping her mind busy was most important. She didn't need to think about her feelings and her frayed emotions. She was exhausted but she knew the team was in jeopardy as well as drained. All she did was sit.

Staring out the window, she realized it was pitch black outside and when she peered out the window, she could see a full moon. It was two AM.

"Hey, coffee?" someone behind her asked. The little man held two cups, one in each hand.

"Oh, my, just what the doctor ordered," she told the man who was still standing in the doorway. "I haven't seen you before."

"I just work nights." He sipped the coffee and stared at her with a strange expression then rubbed his bald head as if he just thought of something.

"Are those donuts?" she asked when she saw a bag held loosely between his side and upper arm.

He nodded. "Want one?"

"Of course, I never turn down sugar." Meara accepted the sweet confection, fingering some of the icing and sticking it in her mouth, licking. "Hmmm, so good. You are a godsend."

"Thanks, well, I've got to get back to janitoring. Just thought you might enjoy a moment of conversation and food."

"Don't leave out the caffeine and I do appreciate the conversation. Stop by when you get the chance. It does get pretty lonely here."

He smiled, winked then turned and walked back down the hall.

Well that was a nice five-minute diversion in an otherwise very long day. What was there to do? She couldn't go home and she couldn't lay her head down on the desk and sleep. She didn't want to stare at the empty monitor. Playing a computer game crossed her mind, but she knew first hand that would make it easier for someone to hack her.

If they found this serial killer, in a few days there would be someone new then she pushed the horrible thought to the back of her head. They would always have work. And the team would always be in danger. She would make Jace and all of them be careful, if nothing else. The quicker she did her job, the sooner they would finish theirs and be out of danger.

Her cell buzzed again it was Jace, telling her they got him and he was in custody and they were coming home. "Stay put and I'll drive you home. Don't want you taking a bus or a cab. Can you do that? I still have that uncanny feeling someone was following us. My instincts are never wrong."

"Don't worry about the time. I have some straitening up to do here." She stared at her pristine, not a paper out of place desk, and grimaced. *You don't have to lie to him. You could have told him how bored you were and in order to clean up your desk you'd have to make a mess.*

"Be home in thirty."

~ * ~

The moon hung low in the dark sky, but it was brilliant with a raw golden color encompassing it. She let her head lie on the backrest, watching the road zoom by. Two days of work and she was once again exhausted and starving. The grueling pace was anything but exhilarating. She couldn't remember eating anything except the donut, but she must've had something.

For just a moment he took his focus off the road and offered her a crooked smile, lowered his lashes then returned his attention to the empty highway ahead of them. "My life is rather at a stalemate," he told her.

She didn't know what to say. Hers was too. She wanted to find ways to move on, and she sensed the best way to move on was to have

Jace at her side, but she didn't know how to proceed. "Want to share a meal when we get home?"

"Sure. We can eat on the balcony. There's a great moon out tonight." He was still staring straight ahead, and still grinning. Then he looked back at her. "You're not afraid to be with me, on the balcony, in all that moonlight, are you?"

"Have you taken up shapeshifting during the full moon?" Meara asked sweetly. Then before he could reply, she answered the question. "Never mind. You would think me crazy if you thought I believed in all that stuff--shapeshifting, vampires, all by the light of the full moon. And any other moon, at that."

"Only sometimes."

"Oh?"

"It depends on the available prey," he told her then gave her a sexy wink.

"Ah, where do technical analysts fall?"

"I only know one," he reminded her.

"So?"

"It kind of depends on the techy," he said. He drummed the steering wheel with his thumbs, pulled into his parking space at the apartment then smiled wickedly at her. "I'll have to see how you taste."

"Is that a promise?" she countered.

"Of course, sexy one."

A heated shiver swept through her. Then a few minutes later they were in her apartment and she was rummaging through the fridge to figure out what she could put together to make a meal. Jace left then returned with several beverages in hand. "What are you drinking tonight, Miss Meara? Wine or beer?"

"White wine if you have it, thank you, Mr. Jace," she said tiredly. "Can you cook an omelet? I have eggs and a few vegies, tomato, green pepper and some parmesan cheese in the fridge."

"Of course, I'm a very good cook." He set the wine and beer on the table, and proceeded to prove his statement true.

"I'm certainly glad you know your way around a stove," she told him, pouring the wine and opening the beer he'd indicated he wanted.

"And you don't cook?"

"I never learned. I can bake cookies and open cereal boxes. Of course I can use the microwave." She moved out to the balcony and slowly scanned the beach, wondering if she would see the jaguar. There had been no reports of missing jaguars when she'd googled the question.

Looking skyward, she felt the warm breeze touch her, and she was instantly aware of the moon. It was very low in the sky, glowing with a soft shimmer over the water. The sound of the ocean waves hitting the shoreline eased the tension in her shoulders. She imagined Jace massaging her back and neck muscles.

Meara could see the lights of the homes that dotted the shoreline. It was a beautiful site, stunning. And she felt as if in this moment they were all alone within it. There was nothing to see except for the lights on the shore, the velvet darkness of the sky and the beauty of the moon and the stars. And there was the water, too, seemingly eternal. The shoreline held the only touch of civilization.

She perched on the balcony chair, and in another moment Jace was beside her. He sat down in the opposite chair so they weren't touching, and yet they weren't very far apart. Electric tensions seemed to zap between them. He offered a silent toast and she reciprocated, holding her glass of wine in the air. He set the plates of omelet on the table as well as the forks.

"What a stunning night," he murmured.

She nodded, watching the stars. "Where would you be, Jace, if you weren't here?" she asked him impulsively.

"That doesn't make sense," he said softly.

"If you weren't with the bureau and you didn't feel responsible for me, where would you be tonight?"

"I want to be with you, but if you weren't part of my life, right now, I'd be on a long run in the hills then I'd find my bed and sleep the day away."

"Is that your favorite past time, running?" she asked.

He shrugged. "Well, I suppose. I run when I want to think, when I want to feel free and when I need to release tension. Sometimes when a case is finished, I will take to the hills and stay for a couple of days."

"What if there are new cases?"

"Leia seems to understand I'll pick up on the call. I've never missed a meeting. I've been late a couple of times. But I never stay away unless I have personal time and I've notified them."

"I see." Meara looked back to the ocean and the lights. What did she like to do most? She had no hobbies, nothing. Her life was the computer.

He smiled. "I have personal time and I did tell them I was using it and not to call tomorrow. If there is a case, I will join them in two days."

"So, if it weren't for me, you would disappear for two days? Are you going to disappear when you leave me tonight?"

"Maybe, but I'd come back before dawn." He finished his eggs and set the plate aside, stretching his arms across the seat and sitting back. "Changing this up, where would you be?"

"I think you know. I would still be in that cubicle with lights buzzing and computers crashing. And I'd be huddled in that little corner, crying and wishing I were some place else."

"You would have moved on."

"I don't know. I don't have any answers except that I'm a survivor, and I most likely would have found a new home. But I would still feel empty inside."

Meara ate her last bite, feeling a bit of frustration rising. She had needed to move on and to put the past in the past where it belonged. She didn't want to talk about this now or ever, she suddenly realized. Then anger surged to the forefront. "I don't want to think about it. It was the worst time of my life."

"I'm sorry."

It was a mistake to show her anger and frustration. A mistake to give away the tiniest emotion--because he was up and on his feet too, and starting for her.

"Dammit, I just want to know who you are and how you feel about things. I want to understand how you think."

Moisture welling in her eyes, she spun around and grabbed the plates and started back to the kitchen. He was right on her heels. Tears slipped down her cheeks, but her hands were full and she couldn't wipe them away. She didn't want him to see her cry. Vulnerable was not how she planned to present herself. She was strong and independent, damn it. She could take care of herself. She didn't need Jace McKenna. She didn't need anyone. She didn't want to feel anything for anyone.

"Meara, please don't walk away from me. I'm trying to talk to you."

"I can't bear it. I thought about my past for the last two days. For the last two days and nights when I had no one to talk to except a five minute conversation with the night janitor.

Jace wasn't going to leave her, he was right behind her, watching her every move. She'd meant to wash the plates, but he was too close so she hurried.

And he was still right behind her. He was going to touch her. She turned, her fingers clenching the plates, staring at him. "I can't think about them, not right now, maybe tomorrow. Oh, I forgot you were going to the hills. I can be alone. I'll be fine. God, I'm rambling again."

"I'm not going anywhere unless it's next door." He stepped toward her and she knew he was going to touch her. That was when she made a ridiculous mistake. She stepped backward one too many times and she was cornered, her back against the wall with nowhere to hide. She wanted to become invisible, perhaps shrink into the wall where he couldn't see her.

He took the plates from her hands. Reminded of the first time she saw him, gun in hand, flashlight pointing at her, she started to tremble. She didn't like the memories resurfacing. And more than anything else she felt like a complete idiot. Why shouldn't he want to learn about her past even if it was just friendly conversation? He'd done nothing impolite. Once again the fear of becoming exposed welled inside.

"Meara?"

She heard the concern in his voice. "I have secrets too. Secrets I'm not ready to talk about, at least not this soon. "

She swallowed the lump in her throat. "You have secrets?"

"Everyone does." He shrugged then looked away for a moment before turning his attention back to her.

Jace didn't take his gaze from her. And he stood far enough away she could scoot around him if she wanted too. She felt the distance he was allowing her, giving her space.

"I didn't know." She told him, but a rise of panic welled up inside and she started coughing. She slid away and grabbing a glass, let the water from the tap fill it then she drank deeply. She felt his hand on her back, patting her as if that would stop the coughing fit.

She turned and put a hand to his chest. "I'm exhausted and I'm sure you are too. I'm going to take a shower then go to bed. And I suggest you do the same or go run or whatever you need to work off the tension of the job and me and anything else. I don't want to presume too much. Then I think we could talk in the morning. I might not be quite so edgy. It's my fault. I'm sure you can see your way out."

Without another word she turned and fled down the hall to the bathroom. After shutting and locking the door, she peeled off her clothing and stepped into the hot soothing shower. She had two days of sweat and grime built up on her, and she needed to wash that and all her fears away.

Washing away the dirt was easy, but she could never wash away the memories of her family or of Jace McKenna.

Diligently, she scrubbed her hair and lathered her body. Then she leaned against the walls and just let the water run over her. She didn't know what had made her so jumpy and jittery. The nervousness had to come from pure exhaustion. There were things simmering between her and Jace tonight, and, dear lord, she wanted to explore them but she was also terrified. The last thing she needed in her life was to fall in love with someone and have them ripped away from her.

He has secrets too.

She had thought he was an open book with nothing to hide. She had to remember everyone had a secret. What was his?

But all she seemed to be able to remember was the way he could touch her heart. How she loved the sound of his voice, how she longed to be more to him than the girl next door.

Abruptly, she turned off the water and groped for a towel on the nearby rack. Then she dried herself briskly and walked into her bedroom to find a nightgown. Thinking of the black cat on her bed, she meant to find the most flannel grandmotherly-like gown in her closet. Rummaging through everything in her closet and her dresser, she found nothing remotely resembling something the elderly would wear.

She stared blankly at her choices, telling herself neither the jaguar or Jace was going to show up in her bedroom tonight, and the black cat on her bed was just some strange dream she had because she was exhausted to the extreme.

She stood, perplexed, certain she wanted to wear armor to bed just in case and finding nothing remotely resembling armor. Then she looked at the door and exhaled with a certain relief because she had a terry robe hanging there. It wasn't steel but it was better than the flimsy night things she usually wore. In fact, lots of women probably felt fairly well covered in a floor-length terry robe.

But they were women who hadn't woken up to a two hundred fifty pound jaguar snuggled next to them and the ties of their negligee shredded as if the jaguar had...

She stared at the bed then down the hall. She told herself to climb into bed and fall asleep. But she couldn't. She walked to the balcony doors and locked them. Then she checked the front doors and all of the windows.

Meara flopped down on the bed but couldn't close her eyes. It was hot and stuffy in the room. She couldn't sleep this way. She had to have air.

She stood up, resigned, found her way to the front door and wrenched it open. Only a few steps took her to Jace's door. She leaned against the wood and heard nothing. After breathing in a deep breath then hesitating for another moment, she knocked.

Then she knocked again with a little more force this time.

It was thrown open, and there was Jace, in a wisp of a towel himself, his dark black hair slicked back from the shower, an expression of confusion naked on his face. "I don't--Meara--what--I thought you wanted to sleep."

"I can't--sleep. I can't close my eyes."

"Why ever not?"

"I'm afraid that cat will show up again. Any suggestions? Any besides keep all the doors and windows closed?" Like a drill sergeant, she marched through his open front door.

She didn't hear footsteps behind her, but she did hear the door close. He was always as silent as cat stalking a mouse. She didn't sense his presence until his hands were on her and he was spinning her around. Surprised, she cried out. The spinning sensations caused her to stumble. She fell down to the floor and he followed.

She was beneath him and he was sprawled over her, taut, tense, his chest naked and the muscles rippling. She wanted to trace the rosettes on his body. They were everywhere and she'd never noticed how many he had. His eyes seemed to blaze, searing, into her. "Meara," he began. "Dear god, Meara." Then he fell silent. He groaned as his fingers moved into her hair...and he was kissing her...really kissing her.

Not as he had kissed her earlier. Not lightly, but with hunger, raw and animalistic. Openmouthed, his lips moved upon hers, wet, hot, enticing a response from her. His tongue swept her mouth, thrust inside and demanded she respond equally. Then he drew away, kissing her face, the tip of her nose, her closed eyelids. His tongue rimmed her lips before slipping inside her mouth again, so deeply the inferno raced throughout her body. She needed to touch him if only to reassure herself this too was not a dream.

She wanted to feel the warmth of his body and explore the contours that were all male animal, sleek and hard. And in turn she felt an overwhelming urge, the fire, and the desperation to have him at any cost.

His lips rose above hers just a fraction of an inch. She touched them delicately with her tongue, encircling them, nipping lightly. He held still to her gentle assault then swept his arms around her. Once again their mouth melded and the tasting and sweeping and hunger were shared. When they broke apart again, his hold on her eased, but the tension in him seemed greater, explosive. His breath fanning her cheeks, he whispered. "Meara, I'm sorry. I understand it's too soon. It's just..."

Beneath him she lay still, wondering what on earth was happening to her. It wasn't too soon. Yet maybe he had the right of it. Perhaps he didn't want her in that way. She had teased and taunted him, shown up at his door and practically begged for the kiss--for sex. Still she wondered how he could just walk away. It seemed to him the kiss was a mistake, but she'd live with the mistake and cherish the moment.

He was on his feet, one hand holding tight to his towel, the other reaching down to her, helping her to stand. She gazed at him, her fingers still entwined with his, her lips swollen and soft and wet from the kiss.

"Jace," she whispered his name. He didn't speak, and his eyes focused with hers. "I'm not what you want. I know I'm not the kind of girl..." Her voice trailed away miserably. She barely knew him, and she had imposed herself after long days at work. But she wondered if his desire was great enough, if she could seduce him.

"Meara, hush, you are exactly the kind of girl I would want." His voice was a low growl, his words fraught with tension, his eyes blazing.

She tried to whisper more softly. "I'm a freak, a hacker, I've been places and done things I'm ashamed of, but...maybe you might want me. That tonight you might keep the nightmares at bay--and the jaguar. There would be no assumptions."

She freed her fingers from his then tried to read his thoughts. She'd never tried to see into anyone's head before. It had always seemed an infringement of their privacy. But the one person she wanted to read, she could not.

She couldn't go on any longer, not without some words of encouragement from him. She stepped back and turned to his front door knowing she should leave. Her cheeks flushed with embarrassment, her back to him, she stiffened her spine.

He didn't speak. She felt the breeze sweep around her and heard it's soft whisper. She listened to the ocean waves outside.

She willed herself to move forward. The she heard his footstep and felt his hands upon her shoulders.

The terry robe that was meant to be armor slid to the floor, and she felt the searing fire of his lips against her neck. She stood naked in the moonlight, thinking they might make love. She felt as if she should wrap something around her, but then she felt the eternity of the evening and the stars and the ocean.

Chapter Five

Meara caught her breath as she felt the touch of the evening breeze combine with the touch of his lips against her skin. He lifted her hair and kissed her nape, then his lips moved once more over her shoulder blades.

His arms encircled her from behind, and she felt the erotic brush of the dark mat of his chest hair against her back. His hands swept upward, encircling her breast, cupping them gently, his thumbs moving in seductive rhythm over her sensitive nipples.

Then his lips moved down the length of her spine. Slowly his kisses roamed, touching each vertebrae--one by one. Warm dampness seared her skin, and the liquid fire was enriched by the coolness of the morning air. Then he was on his knees behind her, his fingers brushing her stomach, his mouth teasing her buttocks. She inhaled swiftly as he turned her around. His face and hair lay buried against her belly, and the gentle brush of his tongue began to touch her there. His hands stroked upward, over her rib cage then down her arms to settle at her waist. Once again he cupped her breasts in his hands, touching the nipples then his lips caressed them, nipping at them and sucking them into his mouth.

The sensations that swept though her were wild and primeval, as natural as the wind in the trees. She felt an uncontrolled ecstasy so immediate and overpowering nothing else existed. Her fingers tore into his hair, but she did not pull him away. Instead she held tight lest the tempest of her passion send her whirling into oblivion.

He swept her into his arms and strode to the bedroom, placing her gently on the bed. He came over her, his lips molding against her, his hands moving ever downward to rest at the apex of her thighs. His burning, touch moved over her to her weeping pussy. She felt hot and wet and she melted into him.

He brought her ever closer, ever more intimately against him, his finger finding and tenderly caressing her clit. Then he parted her further with his caress, stroking her endlessly. Surges of desire wilder than any storm came sweeping through her and she twisted and bucked against him, moaning softly. Hot liquid fire smoldering deep within her rose until it burst, until she fell into darkness, and sank down slowly before him, spent, exhausted, emptied. Then brilliant lights and sparks of fire seemed to cascade around her. She closed her eyes, still shaking, and embraced him, her lashes lowered. She felt a blush sweep into her cheeks because she had responded so uninhibitedly to his intimate touch that had come so hot and so fast.

"Jace..." she whispered, tracing the outline of a rosette on his shoulder.

"Hush," he said, smiling at her.

But then he didn't allow her to speak again or think about what had just happened. He caught her lips and kissed her deeply and passionately. Before she could regain her senses from the first climax, his cock slipped inside her. He was magnificent, and just feeling him inside her as he whispered so erotically brought her near to a second climax before he even started to move.

Languidly, nearly leaving her, then entering her again, he slammed against her tight channel. The quickening deepened, the sparks of fire left behind were fanned anew. She began to meet his slow, demanding thrusts and her muscles clamped around him.

Her world soared all over again. As he moved within her, he leaned down and took the hardened peak of her nipple into his mouth, and he sucked it hard as the speed of his rhythm increased to a frantic pace. She hung on to him. She bit and kissed his shoulders and pushed her fingers into his hair.

Then it seemed the world exploded above her, and the darkness was filled with brilliant colors. The exquisite pleasure of her body seemed to sweep into his while he held still, emptying the tempest of his passion, his seed into her.

Then he rolled by her side, inhaling deeply as she wallowed in the new sensations and the wonder of his lovemaking.

She didn't know what to do or say as she lay sheened with sweat, glistening in the moonlight. Her experience was minimal and this was nothing like she had known before. Hundreds of little things she had seen on the internet crept through her mind, but she knew none of the words were right.

Was it good for you? It was fantastic for me. Nope, somehow those lines didn't seem right for what she'd just experienced with someone she was just getting to know and care for.

Still, it seemed as if she should say something. Yet she knew in her state at the moment, she would surely babble. *My god, I never thought sex with you could be so sweet, so wonderful, how shattering, how volatile...*

I wonder, is it because I'm falling in love with you or because he is really just an incredible lover?

I'm not falling in love. Will never fall in love.

Perhaps he was just an incredible lover...

His arm encircled her, pulling her close beside him. He brushed a kiss against her forehead and held her. She stared out the window at the early morning sunshine and the cloudless blue sky as silence stretched between them, then he spoke. A husky trembling in his voice seemed to reach inside her and squeeze her heart.

"Meara, I can't tell you how incredibly special you are to me. God, I wish I had met you years ago. Sex with you is fantastic."

She smiled and buried her face against his ribs, hesitantly stroking his stomach. Wishing once more she could put a coherent thought into words.

She paused to keep thinking, "If I had met you before I went underground and turned myself into a criminal, then maybe..." She sighed, because she felt so satisfied. She didn't want to move, and she really didn't want to talk anymore, not until a few more hours passed. She hoped their job wouldn't intrude. She just wanted to lie in bed and experience the wonderful sensation of fantastic sex.

But she inhaled on a shaky breath, "We should sleep. We could get called in any minute now."

"Let's pray we don't. I'd be tempted to tell them no or just not answer the pone." He spoke slowly as he stroked her back.

"You wouldn't do that," she told him. Her heart was thundering. His tenderness resonated to her core. She didn't want to move. And he didn't stir. She felt the lightest touch, and the caress of the breeze from the open window, sweeping over her naked flesh. She closed her eyes. She had slept so many nights on the floor or huddled in corners of old buildings afraid to close her eyes. This laziness and the feeling she was safe was all so new. It had been so long since she'd felt protected as she did now.

She must have closed her eyes and dozed. She was vaguely aware of his movements beside her and a soft purring that in her dreamy haze reminded her of the black jaguar. She wanted to see the cat again, stroke its fur and look into its eyes. She smiled thinking about the cat and the strange sensations the animal evoked in her.

When she finally awoke, the room was dark and she could see stars in the sky where the sun had been. The night sky was a velvet black. She rolled over and smoothing her hands across the bed, found Jace.

Jace was still sleeping. His bare back was to her. The sheet had fallen from his shoulders. She gazed at the breadth of his muscles, and she felt like grinning just because she loved the way he was built. His back was bronzed, part from his heritage and part from the California sun, and it tapered to a narrow waistline. Below that his skin was a lighter shade, and his buttocks were rounded and hard-muscled and very sexy. The rosette tattoos decorated his back in an interesting pattern, some darker and more apparent than the others. She wanted to touch him and trace the rosettes. Despite the fact that she was still tired, she wanted to taste his skin. See if it was salty, if--

He turned his head suddenly, and she realized he was awake. His heavy-lidded gaze was upon her with a certain amount of amusement. He smiled as if he was a cat licking cream from a bowl. She met his gaze then moved toward him. Her lashes fell at the very last moment, as she stroked his skin with a fingertip. He didn't move but waited almost as if he expected something from her. But she was certain she felt the beat of his heart, felt the pulse at his nape, felt the intake of his breath, the hardening of his body.

As he had done the night before, she began to move against him. She traced kisses across the breadth of his back, caressing his skin with her lips and tongue. She teased his spine, up then down, with the moist quick flicker of her tongue. She caressed the small of his back and nipped at his buttocks and bathed them with her kisses.

He rolled to his side, and she was face-to-face with the hardness of his cock, the result of her assault. She felt a delicious power surge through her with an unbearable sweetness as she realized she could affect him as deeply as he could her. But it wasn't just the sense of power she felt as she continued to touch him, it was also the beginning of something she really didn't understand. Perhaps someday he would be hers. And on this velvet night, shimmering with stars, he was going to make love to her again.

She closed her fingers around his cock, teased and caressed him then stroked him with her tongue. She heard his ragged cries, and a molten inferno took hold within her body. A fever began to rule her movements. She tasted his ecstasy, and still she held him with her caress, until his hands were on her and he was lifting her and she discovered herself seated on the bedroom chair. His hands were parting her thighs. His eyes glittered with passion. Then he began his attack, burning her to her core with the scorching thrusts of his tongue then rising to impale her and take her with reckless fury. Cries tore from their throats, and seizures shook them as they peaked in a triumphant climax together.

He pulled her close, burying his face against her hair and throat. "I had no idea how wonderful it would be to wake up beside you," he said softly.

To wake up...

Meara looked at the clock. It was almost morning, and the darkness was changing to an early morning grey. If nothing more came of their relationship, she would cherish this moment and use it as a shield against the past horrors. She had wanted him and she had her wish, but was it a mistake?

She had needed a memory to take with her if this job did not workout. Sex was obviously not an issue. Their relationship was new and fresh with nothing to come between them.

We should get up," she whispered.

"Of course."

She began to rise, but he tugged her back, his gaze questioning as he looked at her. "Meara, tell me, do you have any regrets?"

She laughed, "I will treasure the memories. I wanted you yesterday more than I can ever remember wanting anything or anyone."

"What about this morning?"

"I wanted you this morning too."

He inhaled quickly and seemed to catch his breath. He looked at ease and very handsome, sitting naked on the chair. Was she so natural and easy, standing there in the buff, now in the sun and the early morning light? She tugged his hand, "Jace, I really need a shower."

He grinned. "You look fantastic."

"Thank you."

"You're welcome. So, uh, shouldn't we get a shower and food? We've got to get some clothes on."

He shook his head, holding her tight. "Uh-uh. Not yet. I like you naked. If I had my way, you would never wear clothes."

"So, what do you want?" she asked a bit frustrated.

"I don't want you to walk away, start a new day and pretend none of this happened, that's all."

"I would never pretend."

"Or that it wasn't special, Meara. And I don't mean that in a casual way. When I'm with you, you have to know that I want you."

She tugged on his hand. "Jace, I'm really hungry and I really need a shower. Why don't you go for a run or something?" for some reason she was having trouble dealing with the morning after.

He dropped her hand slowly, and his eyes were heavily shaded as they focused on her once again. "All right, I'll go for a run. I've got some things to think about." He rose then relaxed, able to regain his composure in an instant. "You take a shower and fix breakfast. I'll be back in thirty minutes."

She hurried out of his bedroom and to her apartment then into the shower. She turned on the hot water and let the spray run over her body.

She didn't know if she'd hurt him. She hadn't meant to, but at that moment she hadn't the slightest idea how to proceed.

I love you didn't seem appropriate.

What in God's name did she really want? If she were honest with herself, she wanted Jace. She didn't want him to leave her. Not now. Not ever. And not after what they just shared. Awful things could happen to him. He could be killed; she might never see him again. Every case was dangerous some more than others.

She inhaled sharply.

Love was not what she needed or wanted. There had been so much agony in her past. Letting down her guard and caring for someone was too risky. If she cared too much he would leave her. Everyone left her.

Her heart slammed against her chest.

She was so much in love she didn't understand it herself.

~ * ~

The sun cast shadows toward the ocean when Jace reached the beach. He picked up a piece of driftwood and tossed it into the sea. He really should run then get back to Meara. But the mood wasn't in him. His heart quickened with anxiety and the fear that perhaps he'd moved to fast. How long had he known her? Two weeks, give or take a day or two. But he felt as if he knew her very well. He understood what made her heart beat. And he'd known from the first moment he had caught her sent, she was his soul mate. She was his.

He thought to strip off his T-shirt and dive into the waves.

But he paused, remembering Meara, wondering how he had managed to leave her this morning when he wanted to stay in bed with her. He twisted his jaw, thinking he'd like to take her to the hills, perhaps to the tiny lake where he'd swam the other day and show her who he really was.

What the hell was he thinking? She would be shocked, could be disgusted. He didn't know what he should do.

He inhaled and exhaled slowly. She had said his job was dangerous. But hers was too. What if she went out on a case with the team? If anything ever happened to Meara, he wouldn't be able to endure it. His soul purpose in life, now that he'd met Meara, was to protect her.

Time and experience should have made him stronger. He'd wanted her more last night than he had ever wanted any woman, more than he'd wanted life itself. Just as he had known from the first time he'd seen her, when she was huddled in the corner of that awful computer lad, tears streaking her dusty face and wires snapping and hissing, that he wanted her and no one else would ever do. He knew it wasn't just for the sex. She was his soul mate.

He'd known he loved her, that he'd always love her. The future remained to be seen and the secrets told if anything could ever come of this tenuous relationship they embarked upon.

He closed his eyes and clenched his teeth. He had to tell her because he couldn't go back. Because he would never forget how she felt in his arms, and how he felt when he was deep inside her.

Yet he could never forget how he had felt when he learned he was a shapeshifter. He remembered the first adrenalin rush when he assumed his jaguar form and how his father had helped him with the emotions. He could go on this way with her, never telling her but he didn't think he could live with himself if he never told her who he truly was. He didn't want lies to separate them, because in the end the truth always comes out.

And now he had to figure out what his next step was. They were both opinionated, stubborn, determined. They had no history together, but he hoped and prayed they would have a future. If she loved him, it would be for the rest of their lives, and that love would carry them through the secrets. But did she love him?

He'd had nothing when the bureau hired him. He'd made it through his tour of duty, the G.I bill had paid his college, but little else. He'd only had his ambition and his strange abilities. The years had been difficult at first, and many times he had been on the verge of resigning. Then he'd seen that what he did saved lives. Yes, they couldn't save everyone but there were a few. And he knew there would always be another case. Nothing would end. It wasn't just making a living. He felt as if there was a purpose to his life.

He opened his eyes and stared at the sky and sunshine. It was brilliant and very blue. It made everything seem easier. Dear God, what was he doing to himself? He had broken out in a cold sweat despite the heat of the day. He turned to look at her apartment balcony. She was standing there leaning over the railing waving to him her hair flying behind her.

"Meara!" he yelled up toward where she stood. "I'll be right there."

He ran up the beach trail to the apartment. He reached the door and flung it open, his heart hammering as silence seemed to engulf him. He had somehow expected her to meet him at the door.

"Meara?"

He spoke her name much like a man in pain. Then he exhaled with pleasure as he saw her step from the kitchen, her crazy hair in beautiful disarray.

"Breakfast is ready."

He pulled her into his arms then he released her and framed her face with his hands. He was quivering inside. "Since the case is solved and it's only a matter of time before there is a new one, we're going to do something fun today," he told her.

She tilted her head to one side, her eyes narrowing with confusion. By then the smell of bacon and eggs filtered through the room. "We need to eat first. Did you have a nice run?"

Jace smiled, wondering what she was thinking about yesterday and this morning. "No, I just sat and watched the waves."

"Really. What, do you expect me to workout all of the time?"

"No, it's just that you seem to like to get sweaty."

"We could get sweaty together. Has there been a call from the bureau?"

"No, thank god. I want to kick back and relax. Find a little sun, get a little tan. So what do you say? After we eat, lets fix a picnic basket and go exploring."

"Do I need a swimsuit?"

"Only if you want to get a some relief from the sun." He felt himself grinning and thinking about the way she would look in a bikini. Was she a swimmer or a dog-paddler? Guess he was about to find out.

They ate and a few minutes later they were in his car on the way to his running trails. The drive was short. He was able to come within a quarter mile of the small lake. She had a bag of clothes and he carried the food.

They threw out a blanket half in the shade and the other half in the sun.

"Swim?" Jace asked while he stripped his T-shirt over his head then stared at Meara, waiting for her to do the same.

She slipped off her cover-up and was wearing a black-and-purple bikini, a two-piece concoction that seemed to enhance the perfect roundness of her breasts and maybe display just a little too much of them. The bottoms of the suit had those high-cut thighs, and despite her tiny height, her legs seemed to go on forever beneath them. Her stomach was flat and her waist slim, and the little string tie that held the suit together seemed to enhance everything on her body.

He'd loved her naked this morning. He'd known then she was uncannily perfect and sensual, and he loved the silky feel of her flesh. The suit shouldn't have held any surprises for him, except that...

Did she wear that whenever she went swimming? He'd never been the jealous type, but he suddenly hoped she was never that close to naked in front of strangers.

She walked toward the water and kicked off her flip-flops just as she reached the edge. Looking over her shoulder at him, she grinned and gave him a look that asked, aren't you coming?

Once she was waist deep, she settled down so the water rose, her hair swirling on top of the lake. Then she was swimming, a head high crawl across the water her arms perfectly placed as if she was a synchronized swimmer. She turned over and executed a perfect ballet leg, still gliding across the top of the water.

She stopped, brought her leg down and treading water, she called out, "Are you just going to watch or can't you swim?"

"I'm coming," he said running, and when he dove, skimming the top of the water. In a moment's time he was beside her so tempted to pull the string of her bikini top and make mad sensual love in the lake. But he knew that while they would have a measure of privacy, there were homes nearby. Perhaps a moonlight tryst would be in their future. There was nothing more sensuous and sinful than skinny-dipping.

She splashed him before, kicking away from him. He swam after her, dunked her then waited for her to surface. Instead she swam beneath the surface, grabbing his legs, she tugged him underwater.

They both surfaced laughing. He grabbed her wrist and pulled her close, kissing her tenderly on the lips, not choosing to deepen the kiss for fear he'd have no control over his body. She ran her hands through his hair and kissed him back. When he pulled away, she looked at him with a funny expression.

"I'm hungry," she told him. "Want to race?" She took off before he could respond. He laughed then chased her. She was a fast little devil, but he was faster. He caught her easily then passed her.

He stood in knee-deep water and helped her out. Throwing his arm around her shoulder, they walked together to the blanket then dried off. Her cover-up was on the blanket, and she pulled it over her head. He couldn't help but be disappointed.

"What did you bring?"

"I just rummaged through the kitchen. I have blueberries, sliced turkey, cheese and crackers and of course a bottle of wine. Oh, and did I mention two dark chocolate raspberry truffles."

He poured her a glass of wine then one of his own. "Here's to us," he told her.

"And a couple more days without a case."

"Amen, to that," he agreed. A movement on horizon caught his attention. It wasn't an animal and the shadowed form moved with stealth down the embankment toward them. Jace didn't like this. He felt adrenalin start to push forward. He wasn't ready to divulge his secret. But he didn't like the man on the horizon. He'd seen him somewhere before. He couldn't quite put his finger on the memory though.

He set the glass down. "I'll be back in a minute. Have to take care of some business," he said as the hair on the back of his neck stiffened.

"Jace, I..."

He cut her off. "Don't worry." Taking his gun from the bottom of the basket, he stuck it in the back of his swimsuit waistband. Tossing her the keys to the car, he gave a pointed look in that direction. "Go to the car and wait for me."

"Jace, no."

He didn't want to argue with her. "Please, it would help me if I knew you were safe, locked in the car with the ignition on ready to head down the mountain."

"But what about you?"

"I'll be fine. I'm sure it's nothing but I'm not going to stay down here like a sitting-duck, waiting to be slaughtered." But he had a crazy feeling about this. Thoughts of skinwalkers shot through his head and a chill swept within. The name brought terror to his heart. They were shapeshifters too but they were evil beings created when they killed a relative.

She looked at the keys in her hand and nodded slightly. "All right, but if your not back in--"

"Don't do anything stupid Meara. If I don't return in a timely manner, drive home and call Colton. I don't want to involve the whole team." Jace smiled, knowing she wanted to fight him the whole way. But she'd seen enough in the short time she'd been with the bureau that she was going to do what he asked. He knew the minute she complied. "Good girl."

Unsure of her acceptance, he looked into her eyes, ready for the biggest argument of their short relationship.

"Is it settled?" he asked her tensely.

She grinned. "If this is what you want," she said sweetly.

Her smile was absolutely beautiful, totally innocent. Her eyes were wide and very blue, and her hair was just beginning to dry. It was framing her face with soft tendrils of various colors.

She was being too agreeable. Maybe she did just want him to get back as soon as possible.

It's not so much a matter of what I want," he told her. "It's what's necessary."

"Okay. I trust you."

He suddenly didn't trust her "okay." Still, he couldn't continue this discussion because she was agreeing with him.

He stared at her until she was sitting in the drivers seat then headed up the hill to the spot he'd seen the man. Footprints led toward another road. He found a tiny piece of fabric but no one was there. Crouching low, he kept moving, knowing he could go faster in his cat form but not wishing to risk discovery, he didn't shift. Once he spotted a shaggy coyote but then it vanished. He found no more footprints. He was struck with the idea the skinwalker might have shifted to his coyote form. He didn't know why, but he had an uncanny gut feeling this one's other form was that of a wolf.

By the time he reached the road, all he saw was a battered greyish-blue Buick and lots of dust rolling behind the vehicle.

He watched inhaling and exhaling then thinking. A skinwalker could change into any form he wished. Lord, but they were evil creatures. If this human was a skinwalker, he was pure evil.

Chapter Six

Jace ran back to his car, anxious to move as quickly as possible to beat whoever was lurking behind him there. He wanted to make sure Meara was safe. And he wasn't at all sure the hair on the back of his neck was still standing on end. There had been a few times he'd felt it and thought someone was following him. He prayed whoever was out there wasn't stalking Meara.

He was worried though. He would be a whole lot happier once he had Meara back in her apartment with him. Still, he turned to look at his back trail. Nothing. For a moment he felt better. Wind shimmered through the leaves of the trees, poignant and heart stopping. Once again he turned and raced back to his car, wishing he could shift and be there faster than running in human form. But he didn't dare.

His car was one hundred yards away and the motor was running. He saw Meara behind the wheel just as he'd asked her. She was watching him, and he waved. She waved in return.

"Hi," he said as he slipped into the seat beside her.

"See anything?"

"Just an old blue Buick and a coyote."

"I've seen one parked near the apartment," she told him, her eyes huge.

That sent a jolt of nervous energy through him, all senses keen. "Really? Why didn't you tell me?" God, would his heart stop thundering?

"I didn't think it was important." Meara looked at him briefly then back to the road as she swung the car around and headed home.

Well, he didn't know what to say to her. *Hey there might be a serial killer out there stalking us.* Or it could be worse. The stalker could be a skinwalker. They both knew the truth of that. Lord, but he wanted to guard her with his life, but he kept telling himself paranoia had no business here. The facts would tell him everything he needed to know. Even with all that was going on at the moment, he couldn't stop this overwhelming desire he had to touch her, to hold her, to make love to her. Sex with her was the sweetest he'd ever had.

Meara was music, a sweet beat of laughter and impulse and challenge and never-ending curiosity, always willing to take a chance and explore new things. She was vibrant and made his heart skip a beat each time he saw her, touched her, spoke to her.

Dust swirled behind them as they drove in silence, each with their own thoughts. Finally, she turned the car onto the road to the apartments. "Drive around the building before you park," Jace said.

As if she understood why, Meara nodded. The old blue Buick was parked near a sand dune leading to the beach. Chills swept down his spine, and once again the hair on the back of his neck stood on end.

"There it is," Meara said. "But no one is inside."

Jace didn't like the feelings. Anyone could climb the trellis to her apartment or to his. His gut clenched with apprehension. Sweat beaded on his forehead.

The late afternoon sun beat down upon him as he stepped from the car. "Stay here, keep the motor running and if anyone but me comes close, get out of here."

"But..."

"I mean it, Meara."

"What about you?"

"I can take care of myself." He holstered his gun in the back of his suit. Jace jogged easily toward the old Buick, memorizing the license plate then he set off down a trail toward the beach. Once again he saw nothing and heard only an eerie moaning of the sea breeze sweeping inland.

Nightfall was fast approaching. He turned back and came up short when both the Buick and his car were gone. His heart thundered in his chest. Tamping down every nerve ending and trying hard not to panic, his years of training kicked in. He rounded the corner of the building.

Stay calm.

There were lots of people around. Nothing has happened to Meara. His thoughts churned in his head as he made a quick sweep around the apartments. Cold sweat slipped down his back and chest. His breathing quickened. Then he saw his car. Meara sitting in it, hands on the steering wheel. Relief swept over him and he inhaled a long steady deep breath.

A few seconds later, he was beside the car and opened the driver side door. A scream ripped through the air. Meara's elbow caught him in the chin. His arms wrapped around her trembling body and held her tight. Her limbs thrashed and flailed as he pulled her out of the car, grunting.

"Hush, it's me," he said. "Just me, no one else. I won't let anyone hurt you."

He held her close, his hand cupped behind her head. Her tears ran down his chest, searing him, telling him of her fear. She trembled from head to toe. Desperately he wanted to take away her fear.

81

"Jace," she pulled away to look at him. Her eyes were shimmering with moisture. "You scared me half to death."

"Son of a... I didn't mean to. I didn't know. I thought..." *Hell what did I think?* "You moved the car."

"I just did what you told me to do. I'm so spooked right now I can barely breathe. I need a drink."

He pulled her back to him, holding her head then stroking her hair. "So my question is--why?"

"Just a suspicious man. He wore this long trench coat and what I could see of his hair it was disheveled. He hadn't shaved in a couple of days. Beard stubble dotted his chin. And I didn't like the way he stared at me and the car."

"How old?"

Meara leaned back screwing up her face as if concentrating. "I don't know, forties maybe." She put her head back on his chest.

"Let's go inside." Jace turned her and with his arm across her shoulder, feeling as if he never wanted to let her go, they began their journey back to the apartment.

"I'm hungry and I need a glass of wine."

"Me too, but I'm going to check out both apartments including all the closets before we let down our guard."

"You think he might be a stalker?"

"I don't know who he is or what he is, but I'm not about to take any chances." Jace's voice came out with gravely undertones, not wanting to tell her his thoughts. How could he tell her about a skinwalker when he couldn't even tell her he was a shapeshifter? He clenched his jaw hard, determined to find out who this guy was and what he was. He prayed he was not a skinwalker. "When our places are secure, I want you to see if you can find out who he is."

"How, what do you know about him that I can trace?"

"Memorized his license."

"Ohh..."

They stood in front of her door, and as he pushed it open, the hinges creaked and moaned. His hands were on his gun and his arms extended at ready as he stared into the living room. Cautiously he moved through the rooms keeping Meara at his side or behind him.

"All clear," he finally said before locking the doors to the balcony. "Stay here, I'll check out my apartment then be right back."

Meara nodded then sat down at her computer, turning it on and going to work.

Jace's apartment was also clear. When he returned, he had to smile at Meara. Her head was bent over the keyboard and her fingers seemed to be flying they were moving so fast.

"Found anything?" he asked as he stepped behind her. He wanted to sweep her hair aside and kiss the back of her neck. He needed to make mad passionate sweet love to her. But more than anything else he had to tell her what he was.

But not today.

"This car belongs to a nineteen year old boy who lives in Atlanta Georgia. It was reported stolen one month ago."

"I'll bet the guy were looking for abandoned it." Jace peered out the window. The car had returned and was sitting next to the dune where he'd first seen it. He pulled out his cell and called the police station, reporting the car. If he'd thought the man who stole it would return, he would have left it sitting by the dune where he could watch it. Now they didn't know what he'd turn up in.

"I want you to sit down with a sketch artist tomorrow. I'd like to know what that man looks like."

"Okay, if you think it will help. I didn't really get a good look at him." She shrugged. "Hoody."

"Just do the best you can," he held her hand and pulled her up. Together they walked to the balcony doors. He unlocked them and they stepped forward. He turned to stare at her. Even in the growing darkness her eyes shimmered with moisture.

As they watched the waves lap against the beach, the moonlight was growing stronger, cutting through the shadows of the night. He inclined his head, watching her with a certain wonder, noting the soft play of light across her face then the soft rise and fall of her breasts. God, he did love her breasts--loved the way they bounced and jiggled when they had sex. His cock grew hard. Damn, he shook the sexual fantasies from his head so he could think.

"Is there anywhere you can go--to stay safe?" Jace asked.

"Right here with you next door is the safest place for me. I don't have anyone I can rely on."

"Meara, I'm worried about you. You would be safest if you were far away," he said feeling frustration eat at him. She had no one, no place where he could send her. If it was a skinwalker and if he was after Meara, he'd find her.

She was silent for a moment. "No, I can't go away. I just found myself and I'm not running. I like my job and the people I work with-- even the janitor is nice. Did you know he brought me coffee and doughnuts?"

They both felt the breeze stir, the gentle movement of the wind against their flesh, the coolness of the night air. He stared at her then sank onto a chair, sighing, and knowing she was right.

"Even if running might save your life?" he queried, thinking about the janitor and trying to remember what the man looked like.

"If some weirdo is after me, and we don't know if there really is a crazy guy, he would follow me. Don't you think?" she sat down beside him, her face to the ocean, her chin resting on one hand.

He wanted to see her expression, to delve inside her mind and find out what she was thinking. "Maybe," he told her his voice soft, he gently touched her chin and turned her to face him. "Why can't you even consider it?"

"Because this is the first home since my parents passed I can really consider a home. And I don't want to be forced out. If I left, I would be looking over my shoulder the entire time. Don't forget that I have seen what serial killers do to their victims."

"You shouldn't have to fear this man. So, I'm moving in with you. I'll sleep on the floor if you want."

"It's almost as if you're inviting me to play the married couple. Is that what you are doing?"

"Not if I'm sleeping on the floor." He straightened suddenly and walked to the railing. He stared at the water then said. "Okay, you stay here. I sleep wherever you want me. And you have to follow my rules. Otherwise I'll be terrified for you at every little creak and groan."

"Agreed. And if you want, you will sleep in my bed. I don't want you on the floor. So what are the rules?" she asked slanting him what he thought was a triumphant smile.

"You will stay in your apartment except when we go to work. And we will drive together." He waited for her protest.

"Okay, that's not so hard."

"You don't walk to the beach unless I'm with you. You don't fetch the mail or do anything by yourself."

"Jace--"

"Anything at all, alright?"

"I don't see any other way."

"You sure you want me in your bed?"

~ * ~

Warmth shimmered inside her. She understood what he said. It was just that her mouth had gone as dry as the Sahara desert. And she was very sure she wouldn't regret anything about playing house with Jace, but she wasn't so sure he would reciprocate her feelings. And she didn't know if all he wanted was the sex. Sex was good and she could live with that but...

"I'm at a loss for words," she said softly.

"Me too. If I'm living with you, I want to sleep with you and I think you return the feelings. Correct me if I'm wrong. You're not my wife, but I think you're my girlfriend. And I discovered just yesterday that I want you and need you twenty-four-seven. I just hope you won't regret this. We can be in a relationship or not."

She focused on his eyes, searching for truth, and wondering if he had just given her exactly what she wanted. Or if his declaration frightened her beyond anything she had expected.

What had she thought? Flowers? Soft Music? A slow romantic seduction? Maybe she was fantasizing. And maybe she wanted him more than anything or anyone else. Perhaps she was in a dream and she'd wake up and he wouldn't be there.

"Meara!" his voice was soft and vibrant and warm as a hot summer day. She wanted to melt around it, around him.

"I'm thinking," she said as she felt herself dissolving into liquid heat.

"You didn't have to think this morning or yesterday," he reminded her, cocking his head to the side and looking at her as if he was seeing into her soul. "Last night you were everything a man could dream of."

"Jace," she whispered, her hand on her cheeks where she felt the heat simmering. Her body responded, her nipples tightening. She was wet and ready for him.

"I'm sorry. I shouldn't tease. You've been out of social networking for so long you don't understand everything."

"Oh, I think I understand."

She couldn't look at him much longer. Maybe he was right. Maybe they shouldn't pretend about anything. But she didn't know if she was ready to jump right into a relationship yet. Hot erotic sex was one thing, a relationship entirely different. It would be foolish to play make-believe, even to herself, that she didn't want him desperately. Even if she wouldn't be able to keep him forever.

His apartment was next door, but he was here to keep her safe from an imaginary stalker who wasn't exactly imaginary. Once again she felt a bit paranoid. Maybe she was allowing this so she could have Jace to herself for a little bit longer. So she could feel his cock inside her once more.

She wished this wasn't so hard. And she wished he hadn't been so blunt. Thoughts of a real stalker sent chills down her spine. If Jace were right, this man wasn't just anyone. He was a dangerous psychopath. But there was something else, a gut feeling. Meara wasn't sure but she could sense Jace's hesitation. He wasn't telling her something.

"All right."

He arched a brow. "You agree?"

"I did just say so."

He smiled slowly. She tossed her multicolored hair over her shoulder, turned and started into the kitchen.

"Where are you going now?" he asked, his voice resonant in the night air.

She had reached the microwave. She swung around, smiling. "It's been hours since we ate. I'm fixing us dinner--maybe an omelet. Eggs and vegetables seem to be all I have in the apartment. And just about the only meal I know how to cook. " She cracked open the refrigerator.

"We can have ham and eggs. I'll go get the meat from my apartment," he said as he locked the balcony doors behind him. "Lock the front door."

He returned in a few minutes, cooked and ate the meal in record time. The meal was simply a matter of survival.

When she finished, she rose, "I'm going to bed now." Her heart raced, wondering if this was a real invitation and if he'd show up in her bedroom in a few minutes. She stripped and donned her terry robe then flung herself on the bed. She waited, wondering if he would follow.

But he didn't. She heard water running and the clang of dishes going into the dishwasher. It seemed as if hours passed and still she waited, her nerves frayed. He didn't come into the bedroom.

He didn't need to, she reminded herself. He already knew what she had to offer. He'd made the arrangement and he could come and go as he wanted.

She hadn't thought she would doze off, but she was still catching up from the long hours the team had put in a few days ago. And to her amazement, once she quit thinking about Jace and once she closed her eyes, the soft sound of the waves breaking on the beach below her apartment was like a lullaby.

She was startled when she heard Jace's voice awakening her. "Meara! Meara, the team has been called back."

She sat up, pushing her hair from her eyes and saw his silhouette in the doorway. She blinked, trying to leave the fog of sleep behind her. It was so dark. She wondered if this was a usual pattern--called into work in the middle of the night.

"Get dressed. I'm ready as soon as you are."

"Do I have time to get in the shower?"

"Only if it's a quick one," he told her.

Despite the moon, it was still very black outside. The air in the apartment was hot and humid. Jace had closed the windows and doors. There was no air conditioning and no breeze to ease the heat.

Meara raced to the bathroom and took the fastest shower in her life.

"Come on," Jace urged her when she emerged toweling her hair dry and hopping on one foot in an attempt to don her shoes. Even in the shadows, she felt his eyes wander over her. She looked down to make sure she had everything on that she needed. Yes, shirt, pants, trying for shoes. Everything buttoned and zipped.

"Your purse and keys?'

"Yup."

"Okay," she walked past him and hurried down the stairs to the car.

There wasn't a soul around. No one but them and the rest of the team would be up at this hour. Jace didn't turn on the lights as he pulled the car onto the road. When they were a couple of blocks from the complex, he switched them on. How many times had she made this trip with Jace? Three? Four? This ride seemed almost eerie. She didn't know what the meeting would reveal. But what she guessed is that someone else had died while they played. The ride was seemingly over before it had begun. She had been so lost in thought.

"Ready?" he asked her.

If only it had been eight o'clock. But she'd known from the start her job would have odd hours.

"Sure," she murmured.

89

Before she could blink, he was around the car and at the side of her door. He opened it and took her elbow, helping her from the seat. She really hadn't realized just how tired she was.

In front of the building he paused a second then led her through the door. He glanced quickly at the man sitting at the front desk as they walked to the elevators.

Meara nearly screamed when Jace placed his hand on the back of her neck. She jumped, startled by the unexpected contact.

"I'm sorry," Jace said, pulling her close into a warm embrace. "Come on, baby girl," he told Meara when the doors opened to their floor.

They hurried through the hall to the large meeting room. Hewitt and Leia were there waiting for the rest of the team.

Meara sighed and sat down in one of the chairs that was not claimed by a desk. Then she rose and started back down the hall. "Where are you going?" Jace asked.

"For a cup of coffee. Anyone else want one?"

"No thanks."

"Already have one."

"Okay, then I'm going to my office until everyone is here. Every second of sleep I had last night was not enough. But I think I'll fire up the computers so I'm ready."

When she walked back to the meeting room after getting coffee, Jace seemed to be on hold and the others were flipping through papers. The receiver was between his head and his shoulder and he was loading his gun.

Just watching him go through the motion gave her shivers. She'd never liked guns, and now she worked with a team whose lives revolved around the need for these weapons. Losing any one of them was very realistic.

"I wish you didn't carry that."

He glanced at her, arching a brow. "Me too, baby girl. But we both no there is no other choice."

She shivered despite herself. Everyone here except her carried a weapon. Jace had more than one. He hid them everywhere on his body he could find a spot. She'd watched him one night before he settled in to relax take them off and set them in a drawer.

"If you want, next day off I'll teach you how to shoot."

She backed up a step, shaking her head. "Not a date. No way. I don't even want to touch a gun."

"Okay, but any time you change your mind, all you have to do is ask."

"When Hades takes angels."

He cast her a quick glance then was caught up in his phone conversation. "Colton, yes it's Jace." If he was talking to Colton, where was he? On his way to the bureau? Or was he already at the crime scene?

She could just barely hear Colton's voice but she couldn't make out was being said. "Colton, hang on for a second," he said as Meara started to turn away. "You're going to the lab?"

She nodded, wondering if he thought she was not coming back in when they briefed the team. She would come back, didn't have another choice. She just needed to relax in her world. The world where she could lose herself in thought and the hum of lights and machines.

"Okay," he said distractedly.

She arched a brow and turned her head a bit to the side studying him for a nano-second, but he had turned his attention back to the phone conversation. She walked into her lab with her coffee, revved up the terminals, and watched the machines hum to life--so cathartic.

The site was delicious. She swiveled in her chair to make sure all the screens were up and running, ready for whatever might come her way. She pulled up a few of the best data bases for the team then explored some new ones she'd read about. She leaned back in her chair and took along swallow of coffee.

Had someone else been murdered?

It had only been a few weeks ago when she had worked her first case, when she first met Jace. She had thought about a relationship with Jace then her dream had come true. Exactly what she'd had in mind.

She thought of her future and it sure did look brighter than it had a few months ago. She still longed for her parents, but she knew they would want her to be happy. Jace made her happy.

The fantasy took shape. Oh, but if they weren't in the bureau, would he come in now? Come in as she was imagining, stride in, peel away the jeans, and whirl her in her chair. Touch her, caress her and pull her up so she could feel his hard lean length.

Her eyes closed. He would come. He was the one who insisted he would. He would sweep her up as he had the day before and lay her on the bed they had shared. Against the whiteness of the cool, clean cotton sheets. His body would look so bronze and she'd trace his tatts with one finger, maybe two.

It would be like playing house all over again, playing man and wife as she had hoped. What would it be like if her imagination became real?

Jace walked in talking. "The meeting is about your stalker," he said. "They'll have a man watching the house twenty-four-seven. They had a patrol car going around the apartment when we drove in, but apparently the man didn't see us, or the old blue Buick the stalker left near the dunes.

For a brief moment she didn't respond. Her head was on the back of the chair, and her eyes were closed, then, "It's bad news, isn't it?"

Chapter Seven

Back at the apartment everything was different. Now there was confirmation she really had a stalker on her doorstep. But he knew the man out there gunning for Meara was not a stalker. He was more positive than ever the being was, according to Native American legend, a *yee naaldlooshii* a skinwalker. Eating and sleeping took on a whole new perspective for Jace.

"I'm going to take a look around," Jace told her, clinching his fist, his inner cat growling at him to get moving.

He lightly touched her cheek, wishing he could pull her into his arms and everything would be fine. It wouldn't be until they caught the killer, or the man who stalked her. No one was sure if this was the same man, but according to Colton, the stalker did not have the same profile. He could sense the fear and the terror clashing within her.

"It's all right, don't be frightened. Everything will be fine." He wished he knew this was the truth. But he would take every precaution. "Don't go outside. Don't open the door for anyone except me. And whatever you do, don't go out on the balcony."

Her eyes fluttered and her arms wound around his neck. He wondered what she was thinking. "Just you be careful out there. Do you have all your weapons?"

It sounded as if she wanted to tack on mass destruction to that last question. "Yes," he said. "I have all of my weapons."

"I am absolutely terrified for you."

"Why is that?"

She shook her head then let it rest against his chest. "I care..."

He swept her up and into his arms then carried her to the bedroom, pulled back the quilt and laid her on the sheets. "I will join you as soon as I secure the area."

"Hurry," she said, but he was sure she would be sound asleep by the time he returned.

"I will."

On the beach he disrobed then shifted. Returning as quickly as possible was at the top of his list. He didn't like leaving her alone, but his gut told him the unsub was nearby. He listened for any unusual sounds and sniffed the air. The solitary stillness alerted him. But he sensed nothing and that scared the hell out of him. Instinct told him there should be more night sounds. All he heard was the pounding surf. Not even the cry of a solitary seagull penetrated the night.

He didn't need to run, he needed to walk slowly, taking in everything the night presented him with. Somewhere over a dune, a seagull cried. Finally. He moved further around the complex and heard the roar of a car engine. Then that sound vanished into the night. Velvet darkness encompassed the evening. A partial moon stood guard over the ocean and the world. But what good would it do him if it failed to give warning of an intruder. His claws unsheathed and dug into the sand.

Jace padded down to the beach and walked along the tide line, trying to feel everything beneath his feet. Ever alert for sounds of imminent danger, his senses were heightened. Another seagull called overhead. The roar of the surf still roared against his eardrums.

Seaweed dotted the sand along with small shells. What was he doing here when he could be in bed with Meara?

For a moment he was too lost in thought to notice the intruder. A shadow on top of a dune moved, a long eerie howl split the night. Jace could just make out the silhouette of a wolf. The form was too large for a coyote. Then it shifted to a man. He was pointing a gun at Jace. Springing into motion, he raced toward the man. Trying to turn himself into a difficult target, he darted back and forth.

Adrenalin pumped through his system. All he could think of was to get to the man before he disappeared again. Sounds of three gunshots ripped through the evening. His right fore leg gave out and a searing hot pain ripped through him. Beach and saw grass hit his face as he went down.

I'm hit!

When he looked up, the shadow had vanished. Jace let out a loud roar and tried to stand but fell back. Blood slipped down his leg. He tried to shift back but couldn't summon the energy.

He had to return to Meara. Had to do it now. Licking the wound, he found that it was merely a flesh wound. His mind racing, he knew he could walk. Forcing his body to cooperate with his needs, he stood and inhaled a long deep breath then let out a cry of rage.

His frantic race toward the gunman might have been foolhardy, but it had brought him closer to Meara's apartment. He wished he had his cell and his gun. But they were back by the rocks with his clothes. Limping toward the apartment, he knew the only way he was going to get inside was through the balcony doors.

Good lord, it had never looked so high off the ground. His first leap left him inches from the top of railing and his energy ebbing. He tried again but could get no closer. Damn, he inhaled and exhaled, searching the area for any sign of the stalker.

Readying himself to try a third time, he inhaled long and deep. His leap brought him high enough, but he wondered if his injured front leg could pull him up and over the railing. Gritting his teeth against the pain, he gave his last bit of strength. He was on the floor.

He closed his eyes then blinked them open.

~ * ~

The gunshots woke Meara from a sound sleep. She sat up in bed, sweat dripping from her forehead. She thought she saw a strange animal-like figure staring at her from outside--a wolf perhaps. But it wasn't the jaguar. Then it vanished.

"Jace!"

She was shivering, but she couldn't bring herself to move. She felt numb and so very empty. Jace was out there. He had gone outside to protect her, looking for a killer, so it seemed. He shouldn't have done that. He should have stayed where it was safe. Terror ripped through her.

Nowhere was safe.

He could get himself killed.

She knew Jace. He would tell himself he was trained. He would have to do it. He couldn't leave this to the men patrolling the house. And she knew he would never sit still while someone took crack shots at him. He would never wait this thing out. He could never live that way.

They couldn't live that way.

She sat on the bed and leaned her head against the headboard. It was solid and soothing. She realized Jace was going to stay out there until he caught the man. She also knew he wasn't going to stay around forever. She wasn't pretty enough, cute enough. She didn't have any curves, so to speak. It would be all over before she could blink.

And he was out there...

Risking his life for her...

She really couldn't bear it if he died. No matter what happened, she didn't want him hurt. She did love him, very much, and she needed to know he was alive somewhere.

A loud roar startled her.

At the harsh sound, she jumped alert. Scooting back on her bead as far as she could go, she cowered against the headboard for a brief second. Slowly she unpeeled herself from the bed and walked into her living room then toward the balcony.

The cat was covered with dirt, his eyes bright against the blackness of his fur. She opened the balcony doors and let the jaguar walk inside.

He let out a few whimpers then settled down on the rug, his tail moving up and down. He sounded as if he was in pain.

She arched her brows, staring at the cat and wondering if she should go to him. If it was safe. Good lord, Jace would have her hide if she approached the cat. But it wasn't one of the rules. She'd done everything just as he'd asked. Well, except for letting the cat inside her house. But the big black jaguar looked as if he needed her and he was wounded. Heck, she was more exhausted, but strangely she wasn't as terrified.

"Easy boy," she cooed as she slowly stepped toward the animal. She gritted her teeth against the creak and groan of the floorboards.

Meara felt her heart thunder against her ribs as she approached the jaguar. "It's okay. What happened?" she spoke softly then moved her hand slowly toward him. She wondered if you treated a cat the same as a dog. Did they have a need to sniff your hand in order to sense if you were friend or foe.

The cat looked at her and blinked, his eyes seemingly trying to speak to her. She was sure he was saying, *why did you let me inside when you know I could kill you with one swipe of my paw. But I'm very glad you did.* After several long considering seconds, Meara reached out and stroked his head and he purred, nuzzling in against her hand. She rubbed him behind the ears then stroked his back.

When she brought her hand up, it was covered in blood. Paralyzed she stared at her hand. "Oh my god..."

He looked at her and his gaze seemed to ask for help. "Easy..."

"Can I explore?"

He seemed to nod, still looking at her with big soulful eyes. It seemed he was pleading for her to do just that. With his eyes and ears and even his tail, he seemed to be talking to her. "All right then, just let me turn on the light so I can see better."

Meara began with his head, pushing away fur then moving on. "Did you get scratched by a thorny bush? Or a rock?"

He shook his head and his tail flicked upward.

Her hands continued their journey, exploring next where her fingers had found the blood.

"Good lord, you've been shot!" His roar was not like the first one but loud enough to send her blood rushing and thoughts of escape prevalent in her head. If he wanted to attack her, she would be dead. "I'm going to look over the rest of you. Is that okay?" She'd heard of people who talked to animals and swore they understood. She'd never really bought into that idea until now. Her hands shook as did all of her body. But she meant to get through this.

Several minutes later she sat back and said, "Nothing else. Now what are we going to do about this. You are going to need it cleaned and probably an antibiotic. You have to go to the vet."

The roar that followed had her covering her ears and wondering when the neighbors would pound on her door.

"Okay fella, no vet. I'll go get a rag and an antibiotic that might help. I really don't want to hurt you or make you worse. I don't know if the same things work on cats as humans." Her entire body quivered as she stood.

In the bathroom she filled a bowl with warm soapy water then rummaged in the cupboard until she found a washrag. Insecurities swirled in her mind. This wasn't going to be easy. He really needed to go to emergency care. And what would Jace say if he walked in and found her with the big cat. He'd go ballistic. She wasn't supposed to see anyone but him until this was over. Did this big cat count as seeing someone?

When she walked back to the living room, the cat had vanished. She looked through the house and found him in the bedroom and on her bed, purring. Once more he looked at her with such huge sad eyes it was all she could do not to cry. She settled down next to the cat and washed the jagged wound with the soapy water.

"This really needs stitches," she muttered, her insides fluttering with fear and something else she didn't understand at all.

But then who would look at a jaguar in the middle of the night? And just how would she explain how she came to have the animal in her possession. Even that, she didn't have a way to transport the feline.

Geez, of all the flipin' weird things that could happen, why did she have to be the one who ended up with a jaguar in her bed. When she'd told Jace about the cat the first time, he'd not responded. No he'd just smiled at her as if she were a child as if he knew something she didn't know.

"Well, when Jace comes back, we will discuss taking you to the vet. I mean that," she promised.

Meara settled down next to the cat, lovingly stroking its fur. The cat responded with soft purrs. Minutes ticked by.

"I wonder if you're hungry? I wonder what he eats? Meat, I suppose. Do I cook it or do you want it raw? Hmm...."

She scrambled off the bed and headed toward the kitchen. There had been about a pound of ground beef in the freezer. She'd have to thaw it first but she didn't think she needed to cook it. "Ugh," she muttered.

When she returned with the food, she'd put it in on a big pizza plate and broke it up into smaller pieces, probably a ridiculous gesture. The cat licked it up in two gulps. It seemed he nodded, and his ears twitched as if to say thank you.

She blinked several times, "You need a name. I can't call you kitty or cat or jag any longer. How about Jackson? Do you like that?"

The cat shook his head then let out a soft roar.

"Well then, I guess I'm going to have to think on this one since you can't tell me what you want for a name."

She sat down on the bed next to him, leaning her head against the backboard, stroking the cat behind his ears then closed her eyes. "Jeremy," she murmured then went on to say "Jason, Joseph, Jerrod, Justin..."

"I can't think of any other names except Jace," she muttered, feeling extremely frustrated.

The cat made mewling noises, the acknowledgment of only one of the names she'd recited. "I don't think the first Jace is going to like that a cat has been named after him. Guess it can be our little secret." Jace says everyone has a secret.

Jace rested his head in her lap with his tail twitching contentedly, purring serenely and smiling a cat smile.

~ * ~

Sunlight filtered into the room through the window. Jace lay on the bed where the cat had been last night when she went to sleep. He was watching her, and seemed to be waiting for her to do or say something. She could smell the scent of his after-shave, heard the fatigue in his voice.

"Where is..." Meara's voice trailed off. She really didn't want to bring the subject of the cat up again. "You're back." And she didn't understand the big cat and why he was so tame. She knew what Jace would say if she told him about the animal. If he believed her, which might be a stretch.

He nodded and with a fingertip, brushed a curl away from her face. "I am. I found you sound asleep so I settled down next to you. It's late."

"Did you see anything? You were gone a long time." She sat up, ever wary, and so cautious as to what to ask.

He nodded. "I did. I saw a shadow of a man. Saw him shoot three times. Then he vanished by the time I got to the spot." He reached out to her, touching her cheek with the back of his hand.

"Why didn't he try to kill you?"

"He did." Jace shrugged. "Maybe he's the serial killer. He's ventured out of his comfort zone. But at least we know a little more about what's going on, don't we?" His finger traced a path down her neck and across her collarbone.

Sure, they knew a little more but what good was it? They couldn't even go outside without someone taking shots at them. And the cat was a different problem all together. She knew she wasn't hallucinating him. And now Jace looked as if he wanted to kiss her.

Heat pooled within with the expectation of his kiss.

She heard sirens and started for the window to see.

"There are the patrol cars," Jace said.

Meara looked at him with alarm and he smiled. "It's all right, Meara. They're going to look along the beach a ways and maybe up into the hills where we swam to see if they can find something. The man who shot at me might be camped out up there. Then we'll have to find the bullets he fired. Ballistics might help, you never know." He dropped his hand and rose from the bed, looking over his shoulder at her as he walked away.

Meara nodded. Jace had disappeared into the bathroom and reappeared with her terry robe. He tossed it to her with a comforting look. "Put that on, please." Then he started into the living room to meet whoever was pounding on her door--the team she decided. They had come to her home. They cared about them and it had been such a long time since anyone had a second thought about her. There was that word again, care. The one she'd been hell bent on avoiding.

Sun rose on the horizon. It was morning and light streamed through her balcony doors. She tested them and they were locked. The team had taken over her living room. Before she joined them, Meara dressed then sat and answered what seemed like ridiculous questions while Jace went with Colton to the beach to look for the bullets.

At noon she made ice tea and sandwiches. They found all three bullet casings but not the bullets then checked the grounds again. The team left, but not before they told them not to leave the apartment building for any reason. Meara knew Jace would do whatever he wanted. Even if Colton gave him a direct order, if she was in jeopardy...

She washed the dishes then walked into the living room. It was late afternoon before he returned. He was on the couch. He had taken his shirt off and was looking at his arm. His gaze darted to her.

"What's that?" she asked. "Did you get hurt?" A shiver of cold swept through her. Terror made her shake.

"It's nothing," he said, slipping his arm into his shirt. He looked at her with a sheepish grin. "Really, I've been hurt a lot worse."

"You got hit, when..." She walked to him, wishing he would let her take a look, but the way he'd so quickly put his arm through his sleeve led her to believe he wouldn't take kindly to her nursing skills. And yet... "let me see." She didn't allow him the time to deny her. Pulling his shirt off his arm, she inhaled a deep breath at the sight of the jagged wound.

"It's just a scratch."

"Have you seen a doctor? You might need stitches or something." A shudder swept through her and shock at what she was thinking. That looked like the exact same spot the jaguar had been hit. Coincidence? She had never believed in chance happenings. And if it was, what did that mean? Was Jace part jaguar, part human? A shapeshifter? If he was, would he tell her? Confusion and fear filled her.

She certainly had more questions than answers, and she was suddenly forced to rethink her entire life. "Jace, are you..."

"Went to the ER this morning." He interrupted her then patted the cushion beside him, watching her, silently asking her to forget.

When she was close enough for him to touch her, he reached out and taking her hand, pulled her onto the couch then wrapped an arm around her. She snuggled into his embrace, his warmth searing her with its intensity.

~ * ~

He swept her up and into his arms then carried her to the bed. Her clothes as did his found the floor. He set her down gently then settled down beside her. He remembered exactly when she fell asleep the night before. She had been stroking his fur and scratching him behind the ears. It was almost all he could do to stop himself from shifting back into human form.

At the moment he had no intention of making love to her. The danger was too apparent and imminent. He lay in the comfort of the bed, tired but not sleeping, feeling the luxury of the sheets after a night on the prowl, then settled next to her waiting for her to sleep so he could take another look at the flesh wound.

She scooted toward him. He turned to her. She came even closer. His heart rate exploded, leaving his pulse racing.

Jace slipped an arm around her and smelled the sweet scent of vanilla in her hair and skin. He wasn't going to make love to her... It wasn't going to happen again until he could figure out how to tell her his secret.

But good lord, she felt like heaven in his arms.

He stroked the softness of her upper arms. Her back fit daringly against his chest, and her derriere was right up against his rapidly hardening cock. He should push her away. He really shouldn't have sex with her until she knew the truth.

How many times did he have to tell himself before he believed it?

"Meara," he whispered softly, kind of hoping she might be asleep.

"Hmm... Do you believe in shapeshifters?" she asked him but she didn't turn to look at him. She seemed tense as if she knew something or guessed. Anyone could put the two identical gunshot wounds together and form a conclusion.

His hand stopped moving, and he could hear the sound of her breathing. "Never thought about it much," he wished... "Why?"

"Something strange has happened twice now. I don't know..." she started to turn toward him, but he stopped her with a gentle kiss on the side of her neck.

His heart thundered in his chest; the need to tell her now, overwhelming all his senses. But he wasn't ready. He just wasn't sure enough of her. He needed to take her mind away from the jaguar. Time was all that kept her from comparing the cat's wound with his own. Perhaps she already had done just that, or perhaps she just had questions.

Maybe she knew they were one and the same. He shouldn't have pushed her to call his alter shape Jace. It seemed strange how she understood what he was trying to tell her.

He set his palm upon her hip, but he didn't quite manage to push her away. Instead his hands tenderly cupped the curve then stroked the rounded fullness there. She moaned softly. But he was pretty sure she was only half awake. Last night had to have been exhausting fore her, the day as well.

He swept his hand from her hip to her breast. Slowly, he caressed her, the alluring hardness of the bud of her nipple sent heat throughout. She moved slightly, adjusting her body to fit more tightly against him. He caressed her belly and kissed the nape of her neck. Good lord, but he ached to tell her, wanted someone to confide in.

It had been so horribly long since he'd been home, since he could be free and not hide his identity.

He pulled the sheet away from her naked body and saw the shimmer of her flesh in the gleam of the muted light. He found her clit, teased her there and felt her honey rush through her. She moaned and pushed herself against him.

He explored the rise of her hip once again, pushed her thigh forward then thrust himself fully and deeply within her from behind. She was so hot and wet. He heard the sharp intake of her breath and pulled her closer against him. Her scent was sweetly intoxicating. The movement of her body was subtle yet wildly erotic. He kept running his hands over her naked hips and buttocks then slipped them to her belly, bringing her closer to meet the force of his thrusting cock. He lost all sense of refinement and thundered against her, lost in his own world. The climax rose within him unbearably. His body constricted with the need, with the desire, with the pleasure and anguish then seemed to erupt. Shudder after shudder ripped through him, and he thrust and thrust until he was emptied within her. He heard her cry out softly, and even as he drifted down, he pulled her to him again, loathe to move away. He stayed within her, just holding her gently.

She didn't speak, but she seemed content.

He smoothed her hair from beneath his nose then watched her breathe for a few minutes before he rose, dressed himself and went exploring outside the apartments.

Chapter Eight

When she walked into her living room, she could see him sitting at the breakfast table. He had changed into a skintight black t-shirt and black pants. Stubble dotted his chin and his arms were crossed over his chest. His gaze riveted on her as she strode in.

He sat up, surprised. "Morning, geez. So soon?"

She couldn't help but grin at him. He appeared to have spent the night awake and guarding her. This couldn't go on forever. He needed sleep. "I'll start the coffee. Want anything to eat?"

"Yeah, whatever is easiest."

"Isn't like we have anywhere to go. How about waffles and sausage?"

"Thanks." He stared down the hallway. A knock on the door caught his attention. "I'll get it," he called to her.

Meara went to the pantry to get the waffle mix then started the coffee and put the sausage in the microwave.

Jace opened the door. A delivery boy stood in front of him and handed him a package. Then he gave the boy a tip.

Instincts kicked into overdrive. He walked into the hallway then examined the envelope. Cautiously he ran his fingers over the package. It was small and compact, delivered in a U.S. postal package. He pulled the tag to open it. Inside, he found pictures.

A note fluttered to the floor. Jace bent over to pick it up then went rigid.

"You've got something of mine and I want it back."

A cold chill slithered down his spine. "No," he whispered as he shuffled through the pictures of Meara. Meara was his, no one else's.

He had been so concentrated on her safety, yet careless at the same time. Telephoto lenses could get anyone into trouble. His breath hissed in when he saw the last one. It was a photo of him in his jaguar form nestled on the bed with Meara.

How the hell...

"What is it?" Meara asked from behind him. She was holding a cup of coffee out to him and smiling.

"Let's eat first," he said, wondering if he should show these to her. He walked a thin tightrope here. She deserved to have all of the information, but he didn't want to frighten her.

She scowled at him. And he felt as if he could read her thoughts. Yes, she wouldn't rest until she saw these pictures. There wasn't anything compromising. It was just a reminder she was in danger.

What the hell does he think? That I'm going to hand her over?

His body was covered in a cold sweat. The serial killer couldn't get Meara. No one could, not here, not at the offices. She was too well guarded. He wasn't going to make a mistake. It was just that the thought of it...

He slammed his fist against the wall in raw, helpless rage. He had to find out who the hell was after her. No one was safe if he didn't-- if the team didn't.

He pulled his cell out of his pocket and called the team. Colton had come in to the office by then and agreed to increase the patrols around the apartment complex and to send a few plainclothesmen to stay with Meara while the two of them set out together.

Jace walked to the bathroom and showered then dressed quickly. Meara had another cup of coffee poured for him and the scent of waffles and sizzling bacon smelled delicious. He sat, wondering how to tell her casually what he was planning. He'd decided not to let her see the photos.

"Were you going to show these to me?" she asked, her smile turning plastic. She thrust the photos at him.

He froze midstride, his heart lurching to his throat. "No," he said, trying to stay calm but his hands shook.

"Didn't you think I had the right to see them? But there is some usefulness to these..." Her plastic smile remained in place while she held up the photo of her and the jaguar. "At least now I know I haven't been hallucinating." He watched the rigid squaring of her shoulders as she took a step back, distancing herself from him as if waiting for an answer he couldn't give.

"I didn't want to frighten you." He wasn't sure if Meara had heard his answer. She had turned around, and as he watched her, his life seemed to flash in front of him. In the long tailored shirt that reached down to her upper thighs, her hair pulled back in a loose ponytail, her makeup all scrubbed away, and with her back arched and her claws nearly showing, she was a portrait of treacherous allure. When she glanced back at him, her eyes flashed, beautiful deep blue, and little tendrils of her hair curled around her classic features, framing them.

"Jace, are you listening to me?" Colton was saying over the speakerphone.

"Uh, yes, yes of course, I'm listening." What the hell had he said? He just hoped that before he encountered the skinwalker again, he could find some white ash to dip his bullets in because if he was right, this man was *clizyati*, pure evil.

"I'll talk to you more at the office, but I know you have to think as if this is just another case. I know you care more for Meara than you are letting on, and that very fact could make you overlook something that is very important. Jace, I do think you know the man who is threatening Meara."

Colton was inferring a lot here, Jace thought wearily. Just a lot to take in and try to figure out before it was too late.

"Yeah, sure, thanks. I'll see you at the office," he said then told him goodbye and hung up. Meara had laid out the plates. He sat down and sipped his coffee all the while studying her.

"You have to stay here even though you think you can do more good at the office. I have a few men bringing some of your equipment here. When they set it up, you will be able to work from home. I know you don't like feeling helpless."

"Thank you. If it's my life on the line, I don't want to sit around as if I am some long ago damsel in distress who has to be rescued by the white knight in shining armor." She took a delicate bite of waffle then smiled at him. Where do you think that jaguar came from? And why do you think he likes to curl up on my bed?"

He nearly choked. Then he had the presence of mind to smile at her and set down his fork. "Probably through the balcony doors. When I leave, the doors are going to be locked, and they are going to stay that way."

"I think that big cat would protect me with his life."

He groaned and bit into a piece of sausage. They heard a car's engine then a few minutes later the bell to her apartment rang.

Jace leaped up. Meara looked at him, her eyes widening with seeming confusion. Then she stiffened.

"I've got to go," he said.

"Where?"

"It's all right. Someone is coming to stay with you, and I'm going to the bureau and anywhere our profilers take me. I'm going to sift through every piece of information I can put my hands on, and I want you connected to me with your earpiece twenty-four-seven." He watched her for any sign of rebellion.

"If you get a profile, will that help catch the guy?"

"It better. All the information about him leads to you. He wants you and the letter tells me he's a jealous man and will stop at nothing to have you."

"That's cheery."

"Meara, I've got to go. I'll be back as soon as I can."

~ * ~

For a very brief and fleeting moment, Meara thought he was going to kiss her, but he didn't. He paused then walked to the door.

A few minutes later, there were two young men in jeans and T-shirts at the door with Jace. Simultaneously they both offered her a hand as well as a grin.

Then Jace was there, behind the two. "Meara, these are detectives Lundin and Baker--"

"Raoul," the darker of the two said.

"Jeremy," the second told her, reaching out a hand. They were both young and friendly and smiling with open admiration.

Meara realized she was barely dressed. Jace was strangely overprotective about it.

"Meara, you need to go put some clothes on."

She shook her head, a bit startled by the tone of his voice. He'd never seemed controlling or domineering before, yet perhaps if she interpreted his tone right, this was a good sign. "Really, I didn't know I was about to have company," she said, smiling both inside and out.

She stared at him then turned. His gaze remained implanted in her mind--the anxious, hard gold in his eyes, the tightness of his features and the fear for her she saw clearly in every nuance of his body. She strode into her bedroom and pulled out shorts and a tank top. Then she sat on the bed, a whirlwind of emotions swirling around her. She shivered but not from the cold.

He wanted her, she could see it in his eyes, but she truly wasn't sure exactly who he was. He seemed an enigma to her. And she was sure he kept secrets from her. She didn't care though. If he had something he was afraid to tell her, he should know she could forgive him anything.

Jace had not seemed a bit surprised at the picture of the jaguar on her bed. She would have expected him to go ballistic over it, but he'd been a picture of calm, controlled male animal.

She rose and dressed, and when she came out, she offered the plainclothesmen coffee and breakfast, but they had just eaten. They were both great guys, cool, undisturbed. Still, they were turning her into a nervous wreck.

She tried to work. She did manage to run a few programs in an attempt to isolate her stalker, but she didn't have enough information. No one seemed to have enough data on this guy. He was hiding in the woodwork, and he was about to spring free. She'd seen the note too. She wasn't his, never would be.

Jace called just to check in and to make sure the detectives were doing their jobs. She wouldn't be surprised if he had surveillance checking up on the plainclothesmen.

She hung up and tried to work again. Jace had given her a list of license plates and credit card numbers. She was pretty sure it was meant to keep her distracted because she vaguely remembered these numbers from a few days ago before everything became so chaotic. Before the shots that were fired. She wanted to talk to her parents, but of course that was impossible.

She was sitting there still trying to work when the phone rang. She answered it and was shocked when a gravelly voice reached her. She guessed it was the stalker or the unsub or whatever they were going to call this man. She engaged the apparatus that might be able to trace the call if she could keep the man on the line long enough. Her heartbeat thundered out of control while she tried to stay calm.

"Is he there?" the caller asked.

She inhaled a long deep breath searching for courage. "Uh, I'm guessing you know the answer to that question."

The caller hesitated then, "I just wanted you to know that you are mine. He can't have you and neither can that damn cat."

"What?" Meara was a bit dumbfounded. Yes, she'd seen the picture of the cat on her bed and had felt a bit of vindication. She needed to think of someway to keep the man on the phone. But her mind went blank.

Then the stalker started to talk. "I care about you more than he does. I can give you everything you ever wanted. You don't want to be with someone who is defective, and a perversion of nature. A freak. He's bad for you. Did he tell you how and when he got that gunshot wound? Did he tell you about himself? That he is different. That he is really two different shapes?"

She didn't think she could keep listening to him. She wanted to slam the receiver down then she wanted to take a hot shower and wash away his filth. The clock ticked and ticked and she prayed she'd kept him on long enough.

"I know what you are trying to do, Meara. It won't work. But you can count on hearing from me again."

The line went dead. "Damn and double damn." She looked at the computer. He had been moving while he was talking. That much she could tell. But he'd been close to headquarters and that surprised her. Was he stalking Jace too?

The man was crazy. Meara was certain of it. Both of them had secrets, too many secrets. She didn't want to think about it because all of this just made her head hurt and throb painfully.

She pressed her head between her hands. Someone could just go to hell and rot. But someone was also lying. Two different shapes? She'd asked Jace if he believed in shapeshifters. He didn't lie to her. Or did he? He had never acted surprised when she'd talked about the cat-- always a bit indifferent. He was lying to protect her. If she loved him, she'd believe in him and that he'd tell her the truth. Patience needed to take on a new meaning.

She loved him. She had loved him from the moment she'd set eyes on him. It was truly uncanny. And she'd never thought to believe in 'love at first sight." All of this didn't mean he loved her and it didn't mean he was sworn to tell her the truth, particularly if it involved a personal secret. Trust didn't come easy for her, but she needed to have faith in him.

But for how long?

She watched the computer screens and waited for a phone call from anyone on the team. The silence seemed to surround her, and as the time slowly passed, she felt an icy shiver of fear. She didn't like it that no one told her what was happening and that she had to sit in her apartment and wait.

The day passed. She thought about calling Jace's cell, but she didn't want him to think she was insecure. Still she picked up her phone and started to dial several times before she would put the phone back on her desk.

In the evening, Raul went out for sandwiches, and she brought cold beer from the fridge. At midnight she talked to them long enough to tell them she was going to bed. They both assured her she would be safe and not to worry about anything. They had everything covered.

She went to bed and stared out the window at the moon and the drifting clouds for a very long time. She listened to her breathing, her heartbeat and the ocean waves licking the beach. Recalled the stalker had taken her picture and could be looking at her through a telescopic lens right now. But she didn't want to think about him. She closed her eyes and dozed restlessly at last.

He was in his cat form. And she knew it was Jace and that he was a shapeshifter. So why wouldn't he tell her?

He returned sometime in the night, but he was himself and the shapeshifting was only a dream or a nightmare. The caller had only made her believe in something that was unreal. Jace was real and warm. He didn't try to make love to her.

He lay on his back, his hands behind his head, looking at the ceiling. She opened her eyes and saw him there. She didn't know if she wanted him to touch her, or if she was afraid he would. She wanted to ask him the truth about the jaguar, but couldn't quite bring herself to do so.

His eyes closed. She turned her back on him. A few minutes later she felt his arms around her, pulling her close.

He didn't make love to her. He simply held her in the curve of his body, and she could feel the heat and security of his naked body wrapped around her.

Chapter Nine

Meara awoke in the morning to the sound of a soft purr. She wasn't alone in bed. The jaguar was lying at the foot of the bed, staring at her, his tail twitching. When she sat up, the big cat rose also, jumping from the bed in one graceful movement.

"I'm getting used to you. Too bad Jace can't be here to see this. I suppose he could have thought the picture of you with your head in my lap could have been photo shopped," she murmured softly.

The cat padded quietly until his head was at the top of the bed. He put his nose down as if begging to have his ears rubbed. She obliged, running her fingers along the top of his head then down his back. His long tail twitched back and forth with each stroke of her fingers while he needed his claws in the rug.

"I wonder..."

No, it's not possible. Shapeshifters don't exist. The stories are from folklore--figments of someone's imagination. She sighed, still stroking the cat. She really should be afraid. But she wasn't and strangely she had never been afraid even the first time she'd seen the jaguar. She'd been surprised and shocked but not afraid.

"Are you hungry?"

She laughed at the sight of his big eyes growing even bigger. She didn't know if there was any meat in the fridge. She rose and walked into the kitchen. Really, Jace must have bought some meat before he left for the office. She hadn't looked the night before. They just ordered out.

"Is raw ok or do you want me to cook..."

The cat had the package in his mouth before she could finish the sentence. "LOL I think I'll go take a shower. You're welcome to stay as long as you like. Maybe you can meet the human, Jace."

She showered and dressed, hoping the cat would still be there when she came back out. She hadn't given it a second thought, but how did the cat get in the apartment? And how did he get by the detectives who wouldn't have left until Jace came home. She just wasn't sure about where her thoughts were leading. And she damn well wasn't sure if she wanted the answers.

The cat was gone when she came down the hallway. Jace was sitting in the living room looking sleepy and exhausted.

"Hi, baby girl," he told her grumpily.

"Hi."

"Coffee is already on."

She smiled and walked by him into the kitchen. She poured herself a cup and came out. She wanted to talk to him, really talk to him. She wanted to tell him about the jaguar and demand to know if he was the cat.

And of course, she wanted him to ease her fears, but she wasn't sure if her fears or suspicions where ridiculous. There were just too many coincidences. And she, a scientist, did not believe in chance.

Thinking about all that had happened to her in the short time since she had met Jace sent her nerves skidding, little electric shocks popping out all over her body. She didn't want her relationship with

Jace destroyed. Sometimes ignorance could be positive. These few days were just an interlude. Fear, his need to protect, all brought them closer together. Once these things were gone would there be anything left?

No. They were pretending. These days had brought them close, but she really didn't believe it would last. When this was done and said, nothing would be left. She had to talk to him.

But it didn't seem to be the time. She didn't have his attention. Although she would tell him about the caller, she had the feeling he already knew. "So you didn't find anything new at the headquarters?"

He shook his head. "Colton seems to think the guy who is after you, is also close. It's someone you've talked to or seen. You would look at him on the street and say, hi. You don't know that many people here. So you have to think."

"Someone I might know. The only people I know are your team. But I'll keep thinking." She furrowed her brows.

"That's all anyone can ask."

"Yes, well, I'd like to think about something else. But I'll figure this out. Somehow," she sighed.

It seemed she finally had his attention. He was staring at her, his eyes gold and curious and his smile wry and questioning. "What is it you think you know?"

She started to answer him, but they were startled by the sound of loud knocking at their door.

Meara arched a brow at Jace. "The detectives?"

"Don't know. Could be the team or just Colton. They want to interview you. Find out what you know but don't remember you know. Did any of that make sense?"

"Yes, and no." she laughed. He rose and came toward her then pulled her into his arms for a quick hug of reassurance, a hug that suddenly turned into a bit more.

For a moment, she stiffened. For a brief second she could imagine him shifting into cat form, and she really didn't understand how she felt. It was all too much to figure out right now. Maybe she was just hurting Jace and herself. Maybe this was insane. The cat was a cat. That was all.

But he'd wrapped his arms around her. And she seemed to melt into him. They were hard and secure around her and his lips were achingly tender when they touched hers. He kissed her gently, lingeringly then he stepped back and brushed the moisture from her lips with his thumb. "I'll be back."

"I thought I was going to be interviewed."

"You will be. I just don't know when. What are you going to do?"

"I don't know. Play with my mind. Try and figure out who I have talked to or seen. I think I'll make a list. Let me see... I guess I won't be writing a book. I could probably list everyone I know on a tiny slip of paper."

"Your two little friends are back, you know."

Her mouth curved into a grin. "Little?" Detectives Raul Lundin and Jeremy Baker were both over six feet tall.

One of Jace's brows shot up. "Well, they're just kids, you know."

"Mmm," she agreed. "Very attractive ones. And actually, I imagine they're both at least in their mid to late twenties. Mature, responsible--"

"And on your list of people you know. Unfortunately, or fortunately, you didn't get to know them until after the stalker made his appearance. You can probably leave them off your list."

"Then I'm back to a tiny piece of paper."

"Yes, but start with a regular size piece. You might be surprised. I want you to think all the way back to the day we met."

She grinned. "Bye. Have a nice day. And you behave too." She wondered if he'd show up to check on her in his cat form. That might prove delightful. She was ever more certain, Jace her jaguar was Jace her lover.

"I don't have much choice. Pouring through boxes of paper with Colton doesn't give me many opportunities to practice my wicked ways."

"Ah, but if you have enough help, you might finish early."

He frowned. "Meara, what are you talking about?"

She grimaced, berating herself. "Never mind. We'll talk later."

"Yes, we will," he said flatly. His gaze stayed on hers for a few long seconds. Jace sighed and turned. "It'll probably be late," he said.

Something about the tone of his voice bothered her. There was a weariness to it, and a desperation. Maybe something more. She felt a cold hand squeeze her heart. Was it because he was distancing himself from her? Passion had risen so quickly, and now it seemed the embers were cooling as fast.

"Jace, I know there is something you're not telling me," she said flatly.

He quickly whirled around, staring at her, and she understood his pain. Knowing she was right did nothing for her self-esteem.

"My god, it's true!" she whispered, backing away from him.

"What's true?" he demanded, following her.

"The phone call--"

"What the hell are you talking about? What phone call?" he demanded brusquely.

"Because he called me!" Meara blazed. "That's why!"

"Who called you?" He froze in midstride. "What kind of phone call was it and why didn't you tell me?"

"Oh, come on, Jace! Are you trying to tell me we've had time to talk? I feel as if I have to make an appointment with you. Oh, my god! This is getting worse and worse. Just go. Go and--"

"Meara!" He caught her shoulders, holding her at arms length. "Meara, what the hell are you talking about?"

"The stalker."

"The man who is killing people and making threats?"

"Yes!"

He rubbed his temples. "Hold on, hold on, we've got to start at the beginning. Who the hell called you?"

"I certainly don't know his name." She was shaking, her nerves seeming to fray at the edges and snapping one at a time. "He said he was the only one who cared about me. He told me things about--"

"Meara, what--"

"The stalker. He said I was his. He told me neither you or the cat could have me, and that he'd find a way to get rid of you."

He groaned and released her shoulders. Then he leaned against the wall, laughing and wiping tears from his eyes.

"Jace!" Meara said, trying to read some sense into all of this.

"He's deranged. The black jaguar that was on the bed? You've got to know that picture was..."

"What was it? Don't lie to me, Jace."

"I can't talk about that picture right now. But I promise. No, the picture was not photo shopped. I guess we both know that for the truth. I've got to have time with you. Will you promise me you will keep an open mind until I can talk to you?"

She shrugged. "I was going to ask you about it."

"Well," he said softly, "that was good of you, really. If he calls back, hang up on him." He paused. "No, don't. He thinks he knows something. Talk to him. See what he says, all right? Maybe we can trace the call. I've got to go."

He started to leave then stopped, came back and kissed her. "Actually, according to our agreement, I'm not supposed to owe you any explanations. I'm only supposed to behave while I'm actually sleeping with you," he said huskily.

"Well, it's just...well...you made me see another side of myself. I'm getting a bit stir crazy in here. I need to get out. I don't want to feel as if I'm underground again. And I'm more open minded than you think."

He laughed. "Open mindedness is good here. We will talk tonight."

"Only if you make it back before I fall asleep."

"It's a promise," he told her. He started to kiss her again. His cell started buzzing. He was already late. After a few minutes, he finally pulled away.

"I've got to--"

"Wait!" she said swiftly, holding tight to his arms so he couldn't walk away. "What phone call were you talking about?"

A tiny shield seemed to fall over his eyes. "What?"

"Jace, what phone call--"

"We'll talk later. I've really got to go."

"No! Not until you tell me!"

He paused. "The unsub called me. That's never happened before," he said with a sigh. "He tried to blackmail me. It isn't going to work."

"What would he know about you that he could hold over your head?"

"I really have to go. It's what I want to talk about with you later, when there is time for me to show you and explain the secret I've been keeping from you."

"Jace--"

"I have to find a way to stop him. We almost had him the other night, but he slipped away. Meara, can you understand?"

"I understand I'm scared," she whispered.

"I know and that's the last thing I want for you, Meara."

"Maybe you should just stay here and let the team find him. Maybe you shouldn't leave me alone. Oh god, now I'm being selfish."

"I have to go and you can work here. Never think you are selfish."

"If you're going, I am too."

He swore softly but didn't give in to her decision.

Outside on the balcony, the heat bore down on them. The day was going to be a sultry humid one. The ocean waves pounding the beach did not calm her as they usually did.

"We'll talk about it later," Jace said softly then gave her a quick kiss on her forehead. She touched a finger there.

Seconds later he was out the door. Meara leaned against the wall then walked to her computer, letting her head rest on the desktop, knowing she had never felt so desperate in her entire life.

"Mrs. McKenna?"

That wasn't her name and it was more than a little premature, but she kind of liked the sound of it. The detectives should have known it wasn't her name. It didn't matter. She looked up and saw that Raul had poked his head into her computer room, the spare bedroom she used as an office. Jeremy stood behind him.

"Hi all."

"Anything we can do for you. You look a little..."

"I'm as fine as I can be, thanks."

She smiled at him then turned her attention back to the computer. The team hadn't really asked for help from her since they found out someone was stalking her. But they needed her help and she meant to do everything she could. If they wouldn't let her come into the office, she'd dig in here and find out where this man lived and who he was.

She began to play with the keyboard and the internet. Soon the screen was full of various files but nothing concrete. She needed more information. Someone had to narrow this down. Her last thoughts seemed to dissipate. She had nowhere to go with the information she'd been given. Meara remained at the keyboard, silent, still.

She wanted her relationship with Jace to last forever. But she'd never really contemplated marriage. Wedded bliss had always been for other people. Her parents had forever. Moisture filled her eyes. She wiped the tears away with the back of her hand. What was it he wanted to talk about? It was something the unsub held over him.

She was going to let her nerves and her fear get an advantage then she'd drip all over the keyboard. She didn't want to do that. Not now. She was supposed to be trying to figure out who the stalker was. But there was not enough to go on. Maybe she should try and figure out Jace's secret.

She didn't want to pry into his life even though he meant to tell her tonight. She stared at the computer screen a while longer then smiled at Jeremy when he said he was going for sandwiches. She gave him an order for turkey on rye and hold the mayo then abruptly leaped up and raced to the balcony.

Suddenly she had second and third thoughts. She moved back behind the curtain and tried to peek out without showing her face. The shoreline and dunes were absolutely quiet. Nothing moved. And oddly there were no people on the beach. She found she was holding her breath in anticipation.

Expectation of what?

Was she just a tiny bit paranoid? Hell yes. Who wouldn't be in this situation? Jeremy was gone. Raul was the only one here. Her heart started to thunder in her chest. She reached for her cell to call Jace but remembered she'd left it by the computer. Meara looked down the hall toward her office. Somehow she felt naked without her phone.

A few seconds later, Jeremy walked in with the sandwiches. "Turkey on rye hold the mayo," he said with a lopsided grin.

"Thanks," but she really wasn't hungry. All of this had her stomach turning in knots. She didn't think she could keep the food down.

The day passed unhurriedly. She couldn't remember hours ticking by so slowly. She reached for her cell several times to call Jace to see how he was doing then she remembered Jace had been called at her apartment. It was possible someone might manage to hear what they were saying, that she might lead someone to her or Jace. But the stalker knew where she lived, and he probably also knew Jace wasn't here.

What was the point? They basically had her stationary and an easy target. So why had the killer left her alone? She was protected, but it wouldn't be that hard to take out the two guards. A little while ago there had been only one detective in the apartment.

She didn't call. She waited.

She tried to be lighthearted and relaxed and enjoy Raul and Jeremy, but it wasn't easy. Then it was finally night, and she pretended she was exhausted. It seemed she lay awake forever and ever, and when she finally fell asleep that night, it was as if she was dead. She didn't hear Jace when he walked into the bedroom and settled down next to her.

In the morning she woke slowly, feeling more exhausted than she had when she went to bed. She could hear Jace in the living room talking to someone. She froze for a second, wondering if he was on the phone, if the killer had called. Then she heard Colton's voice and she knew the team was already at the house.

It was the next morning and they hadn't had their talk. She shouldn't have gone to bed. She should have waited up for him.

She showered dressed and went into the living room. Jace was sitting at the kitchen table staring out at the ocean. Colton was sitting next to him, talking intently, his voice low. The curtains fluttered slightly in the breeze sweeping off the ocean.

They both looked up, startled, when she appeared. "All right, what is it now?" she demanded.

"We know who it is. The team has gone after him. Colton is going to leave in a few minutes."

"Where are the detectives?" she asked.

"On another assignment. We just about have this one wrapped up so they were sent somewhere else."

That did not make her feel any safer. Her entire body started to shake. She really didn't have a very good feeling about this. The hair on the back of her neck seemed to perpetually stand on end.

"Are you going to stay here?"

"No, we are both going into the office. We'll be safer there."

"Then we wait."

"We wait until they've got this guy."

~ * ~

Jace hit the vending machine with the palm of his hand, trying to shake the box of mints from its resting place.

"Can I help?" The janitor pushed his mariners baseball cap upward as he stared over Jace's shoulder at the object of interest.

"Hey, Dave, you can unlock the annoying thing? I've lost enough dollars in that machine to pay for a new car."

"Don't have a key. Blasted thing is always eating my money too," he said as he slanted it a well-placed knockout punch to the side. The machine shook for a moment then the box of candy slid downward.

"Taking that back for Meara?" Dave asked as he rocked backward on the heels of his shoes, his hands stuffed into his pockets.

Jace slanted him a sideways glance. Now the hairs on the back of his neck stood on end. The team was at the stalker's home as they spoke. His instincts were all wrong here. But they were never wrong. He shook off the sensations. To work at this office, even a janitor's background would be thoroughly perused.

"Yeah."

"Say hi to her for me," Dave said.

"How do you know Meara?" His feline instincts took over. The janitor should not know Meara. She'd only been in the office a few times. Since she'd been back in L.A. she'd mostly worked from home.

"Oh, she was workin' late one night. The team was out of town on some mission." He shrugged. "We spoke over coffee and donuts. Nice girl."

This sounded innocent enough. "Okay."

Jace opened the box and popped a mint into his mouth as he made his way back to Meara's computer lab.

She had her own little cubby all a blaze with monitors. He liked to think everything made its own noise but the room was silent. He sat down in a chair next to her and watched with fascination.

~ * ~

She looked away from the monitors, feeling a lump in her throat. Poised with all attention on her and the monitors she could think of nothing to say.

He touched her hand, smiling as if he somehow knew she wouldn't discover anything new. Someone had been keeping vital information from both of them. He touched her cheek then picked up her hand and kissed it. "God, Meara, you are beautiful."

"You're not so hard on the eye either. I--did you know the girls call you man candy," she said softly.

He groaned. "I hate that phrase."

"Sums it up though, don't you think?"

"No."

She grinned. "I'll remember you don't like to be referred to as man candy." Her grin faded and for a moment there was no danger. The team wasn't waiting for them, and there was no place they really had to be. The world had receded except for them. She whispered softly, "Jace, I love you. I love you so much. You know that don't you?"

An anguished looked appeared in his eyes. His features constricted and a shudder seemed to rip through him. Then he touched her chin, pulling her face gently around and kissed her lips. The words he whispered seemed to be torn from him. "I love you too, Meara. I've always loved you, I will always love you, no matter...no matter where we are, no matter how far apart, no matter how many years go by. I just hope that when you learn the truth about me you will still love me."

Her mouth went dry and she felt tears welling in her eyes. He loved her. He wanted her, but he still wasn't telling her he was a shapeshifter. What if it was something else?

Jace had a secret that seemed to be ripping him apart...that he was afraid to tell her. But then he didn't know everything about her. She had a secret to share with him too.

"There isn't anything you can say that would change my mind."

"What if there was something I could do?"

"Hey!" A fist thudded against the door then it swung open. "Find out anything yet? The team swept his apartment, nothing."

"Are you even sure you have the right place?" Jace asked as he rose to greet Colton with a firm handshake.

"We've got the right place, but he must have known we were coming. He was gone and everything cleared out. The place looked as if no one had lived there in months. Don't know if you two should stay here or if I should send you home."

"I vote home," Meara said. "Don't know why I was going crazy there with nothing to do, but I don't have anything to do here either."

"Ok, so home it is," Colton said. "You two call when you get there. I want to know if you arrived safe and sound. This guy is out there and looking for you."

Chapter Ten

"I can take care of Meara," Jace said as he touched the gun he had holstered in the back of his jeans. He had a knife strapped to one leg and a second gun to the other. He looked to Meara, hoping she wasn't afraid.

"I'm sure you can," Colton said.

Bless Colton. She managed to smile into Jace's eyes, then she laughed and he managed to laugh too, though the sound was just a bit pained. He took her hand and swung open the door. Colton stepped back to let them pass.

Meara took one look over her shoulder. "I just want this to end tonight." She rubbed her arms, as if trying to warm herself.

"And I'm itching for a fight. But I don't want you to be anywhere near when it happens," Jace said. Adrenalin pumped through him. If he didn't control himself, he might shift right now.

"You best get going then," Colton said as he stepped back and folded his arms across his chest.

Arm in arm Jace and Meara departed the bureau for the parking lot. A sliver of a moon shone in the dark sky and a wisp of cloud floated languidly across it. He felt a shiver sweep over him. He drew Meara closer.

The lights in the parking lot suddenly blinked off, the world cast in darkness. The slip of a moon did nothing to light the area. It seemed they were miles from the car and even farther from the building. He didn't dare let her go.

Jace felt the twinges of change. All instincts called out to him. Shift...shift...shift. He couldn't do that in front of Meara. If only he'd told her, explained to her who or what he was...

But he hadn't.

And now he did not want to frighten her. He hadn't told her what he was, what he could do. It was too late now. Crouching low, he kept hold of her hand and with his cat eyes, scanned the perimeter. But they weren't cat eyes. He couldn't see much better in this form than any human.

"He's out there. I can here his thoughts," she told him, her voice soft and shaky.

"You can do that?" he asked suddenly diverted from his focus. He saw absolutely nothing, but he felt a shimmer in the air. The murmurs around him shot adrenalin sweeping through his body. He squinted his eyes to see better.

"Yes. We can talk later. My secret."

"That's a date. Meara, can you open the car door? Keys are in my front pocket."

She reached for them and clicked on the door opener. Lights flashed but the car was at a distance.

"I'm not leaving you." Her grip on his hand tightened. He felt the terror run through her to him.

"You have to get to the car. Whatever you do, don't look back. Run for the car and lock it. Do you hear me? I'll stay with you until I know you're safe. Then I'm going to get this guy."

She nodded. He pulled the gun from his waistband then motioned for her to go as he turned scouting the area for any sign of the man who hunted her. Jace followed, searching, until they were winded but at the car.

He opened the door for her and she slipped inside.

"Don't open the door for anyone but me. If I'm not back in ten minutes, drive like crazy and get away. Don't go home," Jace said. "Go to Colton's house. Tell him what happened."

"You are going to be back."

"Lock the door."

He inhaled a deep breath and prowled forward. The darkness was complete and exasperating. He needed to shift and the sooner the better. Darting quickly to the far side of the parking lot, he found a spot behind a tree. Quickly he disrobed, leaving his clothes where they dropped. Adrenalin shot through him as he shifted. His flexed paws rapidly formed at the end of his arms. Power surged through the muscled limbs holding him upright. The chill that had swept his body dissipated as his tanned flesh sprouted thick black fur.

The ear-piercing scream came from his right. He turned, tensing his body in anticipation of the attack. However he still could see very little, his eyes just beginning to adjust to the darkness.

Shadows swirled in the black evening. He heard Meara cry out. In an instant the sound was muffled. In the dim light of the moon, she must have seen something, someone. His body shook with the need to protect. His nerves electrified and were set on edge.

As if he had night vision goggles on, everything finally kicked in, giving him a clear field of sight. Jace let out a roar of outrage that reverberated around the parking lot.

Extending his claws for a moment, he leapt toward the shadow creeping toward him. The thought flashed through his head that he must not kill this man. But his animal instincts surged ahead. He fought for control of his emotions even as the cat inside him wanted to kill. If the skinwalker decided to run instead of fight, he would be too fast for him to catch.

Seconds ticked by. The wind in the trees on the outskirts of the lot emitted an eerie wail. His breathing slowed and he sheathed his claws. Jace crouched as he watched the man change to a wolf. It seemed as if the skinwalker didn't know which way to go. He swerved as if heading toward the car then changed his mind and took a path directly at Jace. His hesitancy would be his undoing. Jace crouched ready to spring. Don't look in his eyes. The wolf was closer now.

With his razor-sharp claws unsheathed, Jace lashed out at the wolf and sent him spinning mid air. He pounced on him again, delivering another potential deadly swipe to the canine's head, missing by a mere whisker's distance. The wolf whipped around and baring his fangs, lunged for Jace's neck, but Jace not only outweighed the wolf, he was half again as large and faster. He side stepped the attack and turning, pounced on the animal, pinning him to the ground. Lowering his head to end the battle, he let his guard down for a moment. The wolf's voice rumbled deep in his throat and he pulled his lips back in an attempt to warn the big cat.

They were locked in mortal combat, each going for the others jugular. The battle didn't seem to have a winner. Jace's need to capture the wolf had slowed his instincts. Unexpectedly, the skinwalker had escaped Jace's hold. He turned to run but Jace was on him. His powerful forearm swiped at the wolf's head, making contact. The wolf twirled and spinning toward the ground, changed into human form. Blood soaked the earth where the man lay motionless. Slowly the man's buckskin pants formed around his hips and legs.

Lights unexpectedly brightened the lot. Sirens blared out and

Jace fought the urge to stay. He had to shift back. Meara must have called the team in. He could see them coming closer.

Hewitt stopped at the car to check on Meara. Jace's rattled senses finally took hold and he ran in the shadows to the spot where he'd left his clothes. Shifting back and slipping into his pants and shirt, his transformation took only a few seconds. He found his weapons and placed them in the appropriate places.

He really didn't know how he was going to explain this. Maybe he wouldn't have to.

"What happened here?" Colton asked while he stood over the man, gun pointed at the killer.

"Is he alive?"

"I can feel his pulse," Colton said as be crouched to feel the man's neck. "Who fought him here?"

Jace shook his head, "Darned if I know. I was looking for him but didn't see him."

"Someone got here ahead of us."

The man groaned as he started to regain consciousness.

"Dave?" Meara asked. "Is that the janitor?"

"You were supposed to stay in the car," Jace said.

"It looked as if you guys had everything under control. Is that the man who always brought me coffee?"

"Yes," Colton said.

"You told me it was someone I knew, but I never thought..."

Her hands were shaking. Jace wrapped his arms around her, and she let her head rest against his chest.

"Meara, you going to be okay?" he asked, holding her tight and wishing he never had to let her go. Against his chest she nodded. He heard her sniff then pulled her closer.

"You two get home. We'll finish up here. And you both are taking the day off tomorrow," Colton told them.

"No arguments here," Jace said. He turned Meara, keeping his arm around her shoulder and walked with her to the car. He opened her door for her and buckled her in then walked around the car to get in the driver's side.

As he turned on the engine, he closed his eyes for a moment. He couldn't tell her tonight. She'd already been through too much trauma. Holding her and making sure she knew she was safe was all he wanted to do.

They traveled the distance from the bureau to their apartments in mutual silence. He wanted to ask her what she was thinking but it didn't seem as if she wanted to talk.

Her feet seemed to drag as she slowly ascended the steps to her apartment. A split second decision had him sweeping her off her feet and carrying her the rest of the way.

"Jace..."

"Hush, and don't protest. You've been through more than anyone should have to go through. Let me take care of you."

She leaned her head against his shoulder. "Make love to me."

"What?"

"Make love to me tonight, please."

His blood pulsed hard through his body. He wanted this more than anything. Sex was a confirmation of life.

A few minutes later, she lay in her white terry bathrobe, her colorful hair spread out around the pillow. He'd tried so hard not to think about what might have, could have happened a few hours ago. He'd thought of so many different ways he could tell her about himself. He knew she'd heard the legends. She'd lived in that part of the world for at least a year. But she'd been underground in a world of her own making. After tonight and the revelation, he found himself praying just to have one more time with her no matter what came next.

Just this night.

And so far it was his. But he hadn't told her yet. At this moment, her eyes were eternally blue as they gazed into his. Her smile was sensual, tempting and so very alluring. He should tease her lips, but he didn't. Instead he kissed her forehead, her cheeks and the lobe of her ear. He whispered against it, telling her just how wonderful she looked in the bathrobe, and just what he intended to do to her and where. He lowered his lips to her shoulder and gloried in the satiny texture of her flesh. He nuzzled the plunging cleavage of the robe, pressing his lips and tongue against the rise of her breasts.

God, but I love her breasts, love to watch them move...everything.

Then he rose, hesitant to tell her what he'd waited so long to do, yet anxious to discover her reaction. He hoped she'd understand and not think of him as strange. He sat down on a chair next to the bed. His heart pounded in his throat. Resting his head in his hands, he sighed softly.

"What's wrong?" she asked as she sat up in bed and pulled the robe closer. She seemed to want to protect herself.

"I have a secret."

She gazed at him then cocked her head to the side. "I know," she spoke softly. "I do too. So who goes first?"

"I will. I just can't figure out if I should show you or tell you." His inside twitched and sweat beaded on his forehead.

"Show and tell," she laughed. "Or is it tell then show?"

He scooted the chair closer to the bed and took her hands in his. The pause seemed to stretch for an eternity. "Tell. I'm not exactly what I appear to be." He ran his hands through his hair searching for words while she sat on the bed, appearing to be holding her breath. *Spit it out...*

"You mean a tall dark and very handsome man with the best tatts I've ever seen?" she asked.

"The tatts aren't real tatts. I've had them since birth. Kind of like a birth mark," he told her, knowing he wasn't making any headway.

"Really..."

"Yeah, listen Meara, this is serious. I'm afraid you're going to run in the opposite direction. So don't talk. Just let me tell you." He inhaled a long deep breath, while he watched her eyes. "I can change shape. I'm what people call a shapeshifter."

She grinned from ear to ear. He didn't have any notion what she was thinking. "Is this the part where you show me how you change into a beautiful black jaguar?"

He nodded as the minutes slowly ticked away. He found he was anxious to change to his cat form. "I have to take my clothes off."

"Perfect," she told him. "I can't wait."

He sighed, slightly embarrassed, and that was a shock. Then he decided to make a bit of a show of it and slowly began unbuttoning his shirt while she watched. The fabric dropped to the floor. Jace started on his jeans, once again moving slowly. He liked the way she licked her lips while she watched.

He was naked and the adrenalin began to swirl through him. He felt himself shaking, the sensation so intense he'd never quite felt this way before.

He heard her gasp of surprise and reveled in the smile still on her face. She was perfection. He prayed as he turned. He was on all fours when he leapt on the bed. Bending down, he quickly and tenderly licked her face then sat back on his haunches.

She touched the tip of his nose then scratched behind his ears. He purred and it was a low rumble inside.

"I thought as much," she said softly. "When I couldn't find traces of missing cats from anywhere around here, when you wouldn't accept any name but Jace, when you found your way inside my apartment and when you had matching bullet wounds..."

He roared softly then nuzzled into her, knowing he needed to shift back but enjoying the moment so deeply he didn't want it to end. Hesitating for a second before jumping from her bed, he closed his eyes and shifted back to human form.

"Wow," she said as she watched him step back into his jeans. It was something he didn't want to do but knew they needed to talk before he could make love to her.

"You knew all along?" he asked.

She shook her head. "No, but I started to guess. As a scientist I just don't believe in coincidence. Like I said. Could you understand me when you were in your cat form?" she asked.

"Absolutely, every word."

"Well, things started adding up for me. As I said, I don't believe in flukes. There were too many signs the black jaguar and you had to be one and the same."

"You're brilliant. I've never let anyone that close to me."

She touched one of his rosettes. "Then there were these. I think we were meant to be together."

"Meara..."

"Jace..."

"But I don't want to be presumptive, you know," Jace said.

"Presume, please. I agree with you."

"Ok, so what is your secret? I can tell you that I have no idea. Unlike you with my secret."

"Sometimes I can communicate through my thoughts. And sometimes I can hear other peoples thoughts."

He braced. "You have been able to hear my thoughts?" He flushed red.

She laughed. "No, you are one of the few who I can't hear. Must be because you have powers."

"My shifting. Thank god."

"Why? Have you been thinking bad thoughts?"

"Oh...not bad. But most of the time I'm with you, I'm thinking about you and me and sex. I've pretty much had a one track mind when I'm with you."

She looked at him as if saying, let's do something about it then.

He was suddenly anxious to rid himself of his constricting jeans, and he was very glad he'd not donned his shirt. She was suddenly on her knees before him, working on the fastenings of his pants. He helped her and in a brief second all his clothes were on the floor again. She kissed the planes of his belly. When her tongue moved into his navel, he drew her against him, pulling her up so his lips found hers at last. Hungrily, they met and meshed and parted then met again, openmouthed and hungrier.

His fingers wound through her hair, found the tie of her robe and pulled it loose. The white terry fabric fell free and her breasts seemed to burst from their confines. He buried his head against her, tasting the sweet-smelling flesh there, pressing her closer and closer against him and pushing the garment from her arms. His mouth closed around the ripeness of her nipple.

Her head fell back and soft multi colored hair cascaded over his fingers and down her back. The sexy sound of her moans nearly drove him mad. With trembling fingers he tried to push the sleeves of the robe from her shoulders. But she evaded him, moving away with a cat like grin. In a pool of light she dropped the robe from her body.

She remained still for a moment, seeking his eyes, seeking something. Perhaps she discovered all that she really wanted in his eyes, because her kiss-dampened smile deepened and she whispered softly, "I love you, Jace."

He groaned, "I love you, too, Meara." Then he moved back an inch, staring at the rounded beauty of her naked breasts and the erotic wonder of her legs. Her thighs were bare and the thin wisp of her panties barely covered the exotic blond beauty of her deepest sexuality. He reached out his hands. "Come here," he commanded softly.

When she did his hands wrapped around her waist and he pulled her against him. Her fingers went through his hair then fell to his shoulders. He stroked and brushed her thighs with the warm moisture of his kiss. He cupped his hands over her buttocks and pressed her closer against him. Tenderly, he assaulted the apex of her thighs, the panties more of an enhancement than a barrier as he bathed her with his fiery wet tongue, delving, caressing and delving once again.

She quivered and trembled then cried out as he crawled over her. He knotted his fingers around the panties and pulled them off, leaving her clad in nothing. She moaned softly, and he kissed her lips and breasts and fell against her core and her honeyed sweetness, only now there was no barrier between them. She cried out sharply, releasing everything to him, her head thrashing on the pillow.

He shook with the desire to plunge his cock deep within her. Still he controlled himself, for she was so alluring with her hair spread in wild disarray, her flesh glowing from their lovemaking, her lips parted, her eyes shaded by the fall of her lashes, and the welcoming beauty of her sex.

He held back no longer. A strangled cry tore from his lips as he plunged deep within her to find a welcoming warmth close around him. Her eyes widened with the force of his entry, then her thighs locked around his hips. It seemed the spark of desire, dying within her just moments ago, rose to life again. She squeezed him tightly, and he stroked and thrust with an increasing rhythm that seemed to bring the promise of climax closer and closer.

She met his thrusts with the arch of her hips. He ground against her. She cried out softly, and he kissed her lips then breasts. When he knew he could hold back no longer, he caught her lips once again and filled her mouth with the desire and frenzy of his tongue as he filled her with the last shuddering force of his body and the stream of his seed. He felt her writing beneath him, and he held her tightly in his arms until the spasms were over.

He wondered how anything could be so good and stay so good, and she could electrify him time and time again. He knew it wasn't the wanting, it was the love, and that desire grew from that love.

Could they survive their disabilities? Perhaps those things that made them special were not so bad. Perhaps they could capitalize on the positive.

He held her closely. The seconds ticked by. She didn't speak and neither did he. And when she would have spoken, he pressed his fingers against her lips and silenced her with his kiss. He made love to her again.

They had to find a way to come to terms with themselves and figure out how this was all going to work. She knew something about him no one save his family in Sierra Madres knew. All he could do was hold her and pray she would love him enough to keep his secret forever.

~ * ~

He was up, wide-awake, leaning over her. She opened her eyes slowly--they didn't want to open. They hadn't slept at all. She hadn't minded, she hadn't wanted to sleep, she had wanted to touch him, to hold him forever. She needed to find a way to convince him she was no threat to his secret.

"You have to know I would never hurt you."

He paused, his breathing seemingly hard and erratic. "I gave you a weapon that could kill me."

"I would never use it. Besides, who would believe me?"

"The press would run with the story if you ever sold it. It could hurt you too, and I never want to cause you pain."

"You idiot," she told him, and stepped back his shoulders squared and he paused. "You dumb idiot. Jace, I swear it, the only way for you to hurt me is to not believe in me and how I feel about you. Don't leave me. That's what you were going to do, wasn't it? Walk out the door and turn your back on us. Don't you understand? Jace, I love you. For the love of God... Jace, I need you. Don't play a noble fool." She paused then added softly, "You have caught me. I'm yours forever if it's what you want."

She waited, and it seemed the earth turned upside down, and still he stood in front of her.

Then he turned, and he stepped toward her. When he reached her, he was suddenly on his knees, and he was holding her against him, his face against her belly. Her fingers lingered over his hair. Then she held his face up to her and she whispered, "Please don't ever leave me. Trust in my love and sincerity."

"Do you think there is a future for us?"

"I know there is."

"My work will always put us in danger. I will be gone for long periods of time. I might not always be there when you need me."

"My work will help keep us safe."

He was on his feet, lifting her into his arms. She stared into his eyes. "Meara, I love you. Catching Meara was the most intriguing thing I've ever done. I knew from the moment I first caught your scent, you were my mate."

She smiled and touched his face. "Good, you can marry me. And Quickly. Okay? Enough of this living in sin. We can invite the entire team."

He closed his eyes then opened them. "Meara, I'm frightened."

Her eyes widened. She didn't think he was ever scared. Not even when he was hunting serial killers. She loved him for his honesty, for so many things. "I'm terrified," she whispered. "But don't you see, we have to make every moment count. No one can predict the future. There is so much evil out there. We have to find a way to counter act that at least in our personal lives.

He walked with her to the living room. "Whose apartment do we keep?"

"Mine, it's bigger. What about kids? Will we have little shapeshifters?

He nodded, "It's possible. Should we start working on them right now?"

"You don't think last night could have started the process?"

"Maybe we should get the license first then head for the justice of the peace."

"Are you asking me to marry you?"

He knelt on one knee and took her hands in his. "Yes, will you make me the happiest man alive and marry me?"

She paused for a long time and watched his eyes seek hers. "Yes, of course." She grinned at him.

An Excerpt

Sweet Sexy Sadie
By Christine Young

Available August 20, 2013
at
Rogue Phoenix Press

Brody grinned then obliged her, pulling out a chair then straddling it with his arms resting on the back. "Now what?"

"Tell me why you were outside my door in the middle of the night instead of home in bed."

Brody shrugged. "Wanted to be in your bed."

"The truth, Brody. Now." *Everything happens for a reason...*

"Guard duty. The noise, well, I fell asleep with the chair rocked back on two legs. Carr kicked the legs out when he showed up to take over. That was the reason you woke up. My apologies."

"So what's the plan now? You sent Carr away."

"It's almost morning. Thought I would borrow a pillow and a blanket." His gaze focused on the over stuffed chair near her bed. "If that's okay."

Sadie tossed him what he needed then sat on the bed and watched as he struggled into the chair. He'd set his feet on the table and he looked entirely uncomfortable.

"There is room on the bed...if you want."

"Too dangerous," he murmured, crossing his arms over his chest and closing his eyes.

Sadie sighed then settled into the bed, pulling up the covers. From the side of her bed, she heard the creaks and groans of the chair as he moved trying to get comfortable.

"We are adults. We can share a bed," she said as she lined pillows up lengthwise to protect herself from unwanted advances.

"Doubt it, but if you insist."

He rose and few seconds later he was in her bed. She felt the heat through the sheets, felt desire raw and primal rise from her core. Sleep was not inevitable or perhaps it was exaggerated. Shifting in the bed beside her, Brody didn't seem to be able to find sleep either.

Counting flowers, easier than sheep, she rolled over. Sunlight filtered through the cracks between the window and the shade. At peace with herself was something she didn't remember feeling--ever. But she felt it now.

Then she realized she was spooned up tight against Brody's muscled abs and body. One of his hands encircled her breast and one leg was thrown over her. She felt as one with the world. She should be shocked, should push him away. But truth be told she wanted this closeness to go on forever.

For a few minutes she rested, absorbing his heat into her and listening to the pounding of her heart. Or was it his? Maybe the beats had melded together to become one.

She felt the kisses across her shoulder, butterfly soft, tender but intoxicating too. Pushing back against him, it was her silent way of applauding his attentions and asking for more.

Other books by Christine Young
Available at Rogue Phoenix Press

Highland Honor
The first book in the Highland Series

Willfully stubborn, innocently courageous, Callie Whitcomb braves a journey through the treacherous highlands to the Macpherson castle. Callie flees from an unwanted marriage as well as her ruthless half brother. Naively she believes Colin MacPherson, the head of the clan, is loyal to her father and will give her sanctuary, protecting her from the vile plans that have been made for her.

As hard and as unyielding as the winter storms that sweep through the countryside, Colin is irresistibly drawn to the impetuous beauty who has magically appeared on his doorsteps. Despite his vows of revenge against her father, she stirs his passion as well as his sense of justice...but to love her would violate all his vows of revenge.

Highland Magic
The second book in the Highland Series

Throughout the Highlands she is known as Keely, the witch woman. She is a great healer-a woman whose dreams come true. Ian MacPherson is a man who puts honor, loyalty and duty above everything. Their lives are entwined when Ian is sent by the Scottish King to bring Keely to trial for witchcraft. He is attacked and left for dead, but Keely rescues him. When he wakes, he discovers he has no memory. As he remembers his lost past, Ian finds that his need to protect the woman who has saved his life eclipses his duty to his king and country., He is a man torn between honor and duty to his country and the woman he loves.

Highland Song
The third book in the Highland Series

With her white-gold hair and azure eyes, Lainie MacPherson is as wild and untamed as the rugged Scottish Highlands where she was raised. Lainie vowed to avenge her rape. Recklessly, she defies English laws and the man who raped her puts a bounty on her head. The man who is sent to bring her to Edinburgh sets a dangerous trap. With nothing left to live for the beautiful Scottish spy steals the sealed documents the English soldier has tempted her with.

When the exquisite temptress takes the bait and runs off with not only the forged documents but the purses of the men in the tavern, Aaron Slade vows to hunt her down and bring her to justice, never dreaming she will tame his jaded soul. When Aaron discovers the truth about the tempestuous woman who stirs his passion to the point of madness, he dares not love her, but desires her with all his soul.

Dakota's Bride
The first book in the Lakota/Pinkerton Series

When Emma St. John received her brother's letter imploring her to escape her stepfather's vengeful scheme and to trust Dakota Barringer with her life, she was willing to chance it. But the handsome, brooding riverboat owner Emma found in Natchez a danger of another kind. For Emma soon found herself surrendering to an unrelenting desire.

Raised by the Sioux when his parents were killed, Dakota had been betrayed once before by a white woman. He wasn't about to trust another, especially one claiming that her stepfather, a powerful U.S. senator, had framed her as a murderess. But he couldn't let Emma's intoxicating effect on him. Now Dakota would risk his very life to protect the innocent beauty who had seduced him with her tender love.

My Angel
The second book in the Lakota/Pinkerton Series

A BEAUTY IN BUCKSKINS

When her father decided to send her to a finishing school back East, Angela Chamberlain refused to be confined to stuffy drawing rooms. Instead, the daring spitfire who could shoot like a man and ride like the wind longed for a life of adventure and romance—and she knew exactly who could give it to her. Devil Blackmoor was a hired gun with a dangerous reputation. But Angela was willing to go to the ends of the earth to capture the handsome devil's heart.

A DEVIL IN DISGUISE

He'd come to America looking for excitement, but Devil Blackmoor got more than he bargained for when he encountered a beautiful rebel who answered his kisses with a wild innocence that touched his very soul. Yet standing between them were more obstacles than either ever dreamed. For Devil had strapped on a gun for the wrong man. And that made Angela his enemy. Now he'll have to choose between his duty and the woman he loves more than life.

The Locket
The third book in the Lakota/Pinkerton Series

The year is 1894. Seeking revenge for crimes against his family, Misha Petrovich follows a path that leads straight to Ariel Cameron's boarding house in Mist Harbor, Oregon. A family heirloom in Ariel's possession leads Misha to believe she is guilty. The locket has been handed down to the oldest girl in the Petrovich family for generations. Ariel is innocent of wrong doing, but her father is not. Misha is torn by his feelings for Ariel and his need for restitution against her father. Knowing that the relationship between them is fragile, Misha does everything in his power to protect Ariel's father. His efforts are to no avail when her father is shot. Ariel comes to realize Misha's steadfast courage and determination to protect her and her father despite what has happened to his family. Ariel's love and devotion heals Misha's heart.

The Talisman
The fourth book in the Lakota/Pinkerton Series

Running from a marriage that lasted one night, Dr. Moriah McKeown discovers the land she has settled on is coveted by determined and lawless men. Yet the proud young woman who once vowed never to abandon her home has second thoughts when her adopted children are threatened. Her only recourse is to enlist the aid of a dark, dangerous gun for hire.

Haunted by the past and a betrayal he will never forgive, Ian Civanovich uses his fast gun and his reckless courage to forget the faithlessness of a woman in his past. He will trust no female--nor will he rest until the threat hovering over Moriah McKeown is put to rest.

Forever His
The fifth book in the Lakota/Pinkerton Series

Struggling to come to terms with the part she played in Jacob St. John's death, Etta Barringer resigns from Pinkerton Agency and seeks peace and solace in a Rocky Mountain Cabin.

Jacob has vowed to discover the reason Etta has betrayed him, sold him out to his enemy and left him for dead.

Isolated in their cabin, they discover their love for each other and learn to trust. But the trust is shattered when Jacob learns she is married to his sworn enemy; the man who left him in the desert to die.

Allura
The first book in the Twelve Dancing Princesses Series

Allura McClellan is horrified by her father's decision to take out an ad in the Times awarding her to the man strong enough and smart enough to win her hand and uncover her secrets. She's an intelligent young woman who takes great delight in the freedom allotted to her by her father. She's well aware that marriage would effectively curtail the adventures she's shared with her sisters and cousins.

Hunter Gray is nothing like the other men who've arrived to vie for Allura's hand in marriage and everything that goes along with it. However, he is the first to refuse to concede defeat and pursue her despite her attempts to disguise her true appearance. It's her temperament that is of more concern to him than her looks. Hunter has worked all his life with the hope of someday owning his own land. Now that it looks like there's a very real possibility that everything he's ever wanted is within reach nothing is going to deter him – including Miss Allura's disagreeable disposition.

The Wager
The second book in the Twelve Dancing Princesses Series

Amorica Hepburn was sent to London to find a husband. Finding a man was the last item on her agenda. With her two cousins, Amorica wagers she can dissuade her suitor before the others. Despite her efforts she discovers a chemistry that cannot be denied. Suddenly she is the arrogant man's wife, pledged to a marriage neither desire. But swept off to his ancestral home above the Dover cliffs and into his strong embrace, Amorica is soon possessed by a raging passion for the husband she had vowed to despise…

Damian Andrews couldn't afford to trust the emerald-eyed spitfire who happened upon his secret. Amorica's hatred of all men of his kind only inflames the war that rages between them. Still, he can not control the intense desire his stubborn bride inspires, or make her surrender to his will until he has conquered the headstrong beauty on the battlefield of love…

A Marriage of Inconvenience
The third book in the Twelve Dancing Princesses Series

A REGAL BEAUTY

When the duchess decides to wed her to a wastrel and a fop, Ravyn Grahm takes matters into her own hands and declares her engagement to another man. Instead of fessing up and telling her great aunt what she has done, she goes through with the pretense. Aric Lakeland is the bastard son of an earl and has a dangerous reputation. But Ravyn is willing to do most anything to keep the duchess from discovering the lie.

A DEVIL-MAY-CARE SMUGGLER

He'd bought land in America, looking to put down roots and end his life of adventure, but Aric Lakeland got more than he bargained for when he encountered a beautiful heiress who made a promise she didn't want to keep. But the promise could not be undone and standing between them were more obstacles than either ever dreamed. Aric had made plans to spend the rest of his life in America and that was at odds with Ravyn's plan of living in England and running her father's estate. Now, he'll have to choose between his dreams and the woman he loves more than life.

Rebel Heart

HER REBEL SPIRIT DEFIED HIS OUTSIDERS SOUL...
She was velvet and silk, eyes the color of a summer storm and amber hair. Victoria DeMontville, because of a promise and a codicil to her father's will, was forced to marry one man to protect her from another. She hated Cameron Savage with a fierce passion. But to hold on to her genetic research and find a cure for the deadly Signe virus, she must pretend to love the enemy at her door, come with weapons of fire to melt her icy heart...

HIS OUTSIDERS TOUCH IGNITED RAGING
PASSIONS...
He wore a mask, disguised as the Phantom, a true legend come to life. Even as war and debate over new genetic research engulfed them all, he would find his greatest adversary in the beauty who'd branded him an outsider and barbarian, the woman he was born to possess, his soul mate.

A St. Patrick's Day Tale
by
Christine Young, C. L. Kraemer, Genene Valleau

Tumble through time...

...to Ireland in 1817, when tensions are high between Protestants and Chatolics and faey people guide the fate of villagers. A lovely Catholic lass stumbles upon the weakly ritual fisticuffing between Irish lads. She falls into the lap of a handsome young Protestant. Family ties, grudges, and two conniving faeries threaten their budding love. But the faeries outsmart themselves when they hijack a time machine that has mysteriously appeared in their forest and are whisked to...

...Eugene, Oregon in the 20th century, amid a property feud between the local faeries and night elves. The conniving faeries from Olde Ireland try to stir up more mischief. However, a warrior gnome convinces the magic folk to control their own destiny, and forces the intruding faeries to take refuge in the time machine again, spinning their way toward...

...A modern day castle in western Oregon. An eccentric inventor is determined to reclaim his wayward time machine and save his beloved wife from her latest misadventure. If only they can travel safely past the black hole...

A Valentine's Anthology

The Lending Library-a fantasy by Christie L. Kraemer
     Faeries try to fit into the human world when the forest where they make their home is destroyed by a mysterious enemy.

Chasing Rainbows-a contemporary romance by Genene Valleau
     An eccentric aunt, an inventive uncle, a mother who wears poodle skirts, and a brother who wears pearls provide a hilarious backdrop for the courtship of a young woman who yearns for a "normal" family.

The Gift-an historical romance by Christine Young
     A man and a woman on opposite sides of the Civil War get a second chance at love after one final battle returns soldiers to their war-torn homes to rebuild their lives.

Writing as AnnChristine
Safari Moon

Solo St. John, a wildlife photographer, is preparing for a trip to Alaska. Suddenly, Solo finds women of all sorts invading his privacy, his home and his office, all cooing nonsense words and blatantly throwing themselves at him. Solo doesn't know why, and he has no idea how to rid himself of the persistent women. He finally decides to beg a favor of his best buddy Nyssa Harrington.

In love with Solo for the past ten years and knowing he doesn't return her feelings Nyssa doesn't want to talk to Solo. She knows if she accepts his phone call, she will not be able to resist the temptation to hope again.

A Valentine's Anthology

Sharks
byAnnChristine

Will Lily and Jacob, best friends forever, find love or will they discover friendship is not enough for a relationship to take the final step into marriage.

The House on Berkley Street
by K. J. Dahlen

When Serenity is asked to find the truth in a forty-year old tragedy, someone in the town of White Oak, Texas doesn't want the truth told. Can they stop her before she finds out what they have kept hidden for so long?

The Placebo Effect
by Solstice Stevens

First, there was the poison. Then, there was a four story jump and the basketball hoop. Jessamyn Hamhill's life has been one validation attempt after another . . . until now.

About the Author
achristay@aol.com

Born in Medford, Oregon, novelist Christine Young has lived in Oregon all of her life. After graduating from Oregon State University with a BS in science, she spent another year at Southern Oregon State University working on her teaching certificate, and a few years later received her Master's degree in secondary education and counseling. Now the long, hot days of summer provide the perfect setting for creating romance. She sold her first book, Dakota's Bride, the summer of 1998 and her second book, My Angel to Kensington. Her teaching and writing careers have intertwined with raising three children. Christine's newest venture is the creation of Rogue Phoenix Press. Christine is the founder, editor and co-owner with her husband. They live in Salem, Oregon.

www.ingramcontent.com/pod-product-compliance
Lightning Source LLC
Chambersburg PA
CBHW060228180626
46813CB00007B/2993